Electric Dreams

by

Katie Jane Newman

Dedicated to Cinzia

Who travelled the writing-of-this-book journey with unending patience!

***

Special Thanks to...

Lucy, for all the mornings fuelled by coffee and pastries, and the all the help when I got stuck!

And...

The wonderful group of test readers who never let me fall...or hit delete. I am more grateful to you than I have words for.

Electric

Having, or producing, a sudden sense of thrilling excitement.

Dreams

A cherished aspiration, ambition, or ideal.

Molly

The platform is packed as the train finally arrives at Bath. I pull the hood of Jonny's sweatshirt over my head and collect my case from the stand, stepping down from the carriage into the tide of people waiting to get on.

I shiver. I've not been warm since I left Cornwall, despite the beaming sunshine. If I wasn't wearing Jonny's clothes, I would have imagined I'd woken up from the strangest dream in which I nearly died and was saved by a handsome man. It would have been a Disney worthy dream, but those dreams aren't real life, they're as make believe as the idea of being saved.

I ignore the odd looks I'm getting. I scrunch up to hide inside Jonny's hoodie and hold up the joggers that are too big for me. I feel utterly desolate. Those that stare would never believe that the outside was so much better put together than what's happening inside.

The inside is fractured, and I don't know if the pieces will ever mend back together, certainly not like they did before. Before Jonny. Now it seems that the sun will never shine again. It's as though I'm back in the storm, wading in the water, fighting to stay alive and the grip of anxiety around my neck gets tighter and tighter. I don't want to go home. I want to get back on the train and go anywhere but here. Somewhere far away where I can forget. Forget that there was ever a Jonny Raven, forget that I miss him so much that I can hardly breathe. Three days. That's all it was. Three days, and now I'm wondering if I will ever be happy again.

A sob catches in my throat. I can't erase the memory of the kiss, but to Jonny, it was a kiss that meant nothing. Nothing. It was so easy for him to let me go but I was stupid to fall for someone like him. I knew who he was, he told me, and what he didn't tell me, I read about as soon as the electricity came back on. I knew his past, the women, the excesses – but still I went there. Stupid, stupid Molly.

I handed myself to him on a plate and begged him to ask me to stay but still he said no. I've never made myself vulnerable like that, not since Corey died and now, my pride is somewhere in Cornwall, and I have another person to miss. My heart is heavier because of it.

I sigh and put my ticket into the barrier to exit the station. I don't want to go home. Paul used to be a safe place, but nothing remains of the relationship we had once. That hurts too. I always thought he was on my side, but I don't think he ever was and the harsh reality of that has made a mockery of our life together. Everything has changed and I'm not ready for it. I thought change was supposed to be quiet and calm, just creeping up and moving life forward without any disruption but this change is too loud for me. I want to put my hands over my ears and not listen. Usually I have a plan, a direction, but there isn't one, not this time. I have nowhere to go and no idea what is coming next.

I want to believe that how I feel for Jonny is just circumstance, because we were thrown together in the storm, and he gave me shelter. It was the confusion of the isolation, nothing more than that, but even when I utter the words under my breath, they sound alien. Whatever I try to believe, I have to accept that he is a rock star, and he has the perfect rock star wife, who is everything I'm not. I'm sure they'll be ok now that he has money. They can move back to London and live the life they had before it went wrong for him. He won't think of me. Why would he? He has had hundreds of women, and I am just one of the many. I hate that I want him and Chelsea to not be ok. I hate that I want him to feel as shit as me.

I walk out of the station and into the cocktail bar a few hundred yards from the entrance. I should be getting the bus and besides, it's too early for a drink but fuck it, I need it. I can't go home yet.

Paul has been ringing me endlessly, but I've sent the calls to voicemail. I don't know what to say to him and I'm dreading walking in through the door and him being...him. Paul will throw his arms around me, say 'surely it wasn't that bad, Moll,' talk about his shit then try and get me into bed. It happens every time we argue. He will never understand, and it will somehow end up being all my fault.

Like always.

The bar is cool, the light dim and the music is the funky sort that one would expect in a cocktail bar. It's not the right music for me, it's not loud or angry enough – some sort of aggressive eighties rock music is needed rather than the plinky plonk of the funk. I want something to obliterate the thoughts that spin around and around in my head that are sending me crazy, but there is nowhere to get that sort of music on a sunny afternoon in town. I drop my bag on the bar and sit up on the black leather bar stool. The barman puts down the glass he's polishing and seems to almost slide up to me.

"Hello." He says, laying a napkin in front of me and putting a small glass dish of nuts on top of it. "What can I get you."

What, indeed.

"Something with brandy in it."

"Brandy?"

I shrug, "medicinal."

"Oh, like that, is it?"

I nod.

"I'll make you a Metropolitan." I must look at him blankly because he says, "it's a brandy cocktail, guaranteed to make you feel better."

"Is it?"

"Definitely." He grins and I smile back, watching as he takes bottles from the shelves and pours ice into a glass. "It will right all wrongs."

I wish it could. I wish it could miraculously send me back to the hours before the storm and for me to have stayed in the safety of my budget hotel or even better, just stayed home. Then I would never have known that there was a sad, lonely rock star living in self-imposed solitude nor that my relationship was a bag of shit. Not knowing would have been so much better than this. This horrible, anguished, cold emptiness. What was I thinking, asking Jonny to ask me to stay? Of course he wouldn't, he had a marriage to save. Damn it. What a mistake. A mistake to kiss him, a mistake to put myself out there for rejection, a mistake to feel anything at all.

My phone rings and I pull it from my bag. It's Paul. Again. I stare at it for a moment, then press answer.

"Hello." I watch as the barman bangs the shaker over the glass and begins an exuberant display of mixing.

"Are you back?" No hello. What was I expecting?

"Yes."

"Where are you then?"

"I've just got off the train."

"You on your way home?" Paul asks, although he sounds distant, as though he's not listening to me.

"Soon."

"Soon? How soon?"

"Why? What are you doing?" I ask, mouthing 'thank you' at the barman who puts my drink down with a flourish.

"I'm meant to be meeting the lads but wanted to see you first."

"I thought you were meeting them yesterday?"

"I did. You were going to be away all week, I made plans."

I pick up my glass and sip it. It tastes sweet, like a warm syrup. "Oh."

"You're being weird." Paul says crossly. "Why didn't you come straight home? Why does it sound like you're in a bar?"

"Because I am."

"And you're moaning about my plans?"

"I haven't moaned. I just asked..." I get the familiar sinking feeling as though I've done something wrong. I'd gotten used to that feeling since I changed my career, and it's only now that I'm really aware of how draining it is. Except this time the feeling is deserved. I have done something wrong. I fell in love with someone else. Despite priding myself on my morals, I cheated. It may have been just a kiss, and probably forgivable, but there was so much behind the kiss that made it more. Much more. For me at least. Jonny obviously didn't care. He didn't want me to stay. My gut twists again and the cocktail in my belly doesn't sit well. I put the back of my hand to my mouth.

"So, why are you in a bar?"

"I wanted a drink. It was a long journey." Long and traumatic and filled with such desperate sadness I just wanted to get drunk and pretend it never happened.

"We have drink at home."

"Paul." I snap. "I don't have to justify my decisions to you. I'll be home when I'm home."

"Alright paddy pants," he sing-songs in his 'stop being so silly Molly' voice. "As long as you're safe. Do you want me cancel my plans? We could have a takeaway and watch the telly, maybe have an early night." The leer in his voice makes it clear what he's after.

I sigh and nurse the cocktail between my hands. The realisation that the conversation with Paul needs to be today makes going home even harder.

"Moll?"

"No, it's fine. You can go out."

"Come home then. We can have a quickie before I go."

"I'll be there when I get there." I say, taking a sip of the drink.

"You can't still be cross with me, for a simple mistake." He laughs but it doesn't sound real.

"I'm not talking about it now, Paul. We can talk at home."

"Well, don't be long, Moll, I'm being picked up at seven."

I cancel the call and pull the picture of Jonny from my bag. I wonder what he's doing. I was so sure he felt the same as me, but I got it completely wrong. *Molly, I've told you how much I hurt people and I'm not going to do that to you.* I put my fingers onto my lips. They still burn from the feel of Jonny's lips. I've never had a kiss like it, a kiss so mind-blowing that all sense of time and space was lost. I used to think Paul and I were a good match, before it all started to fall apart, but when Jonny kissed me there was no question that he was the one I had been waiting for my entire life. When our bodies met it felt as though the puzzle was finally complete because he was the final piece. But fairy tales aren't real, and the one perfect moment couldn't last. Now I'm back in the cold and that one moment withered into dust.

I wonder if the women who have come before me felt this way. Foolish. Bereft. Lost. Alone. Did they feel that they were the only woman in the world for him? Did they fit with him too? I feel sad for them, that they may have ended up with the same squirm of humiliation as I have. *I break people Molly.* Yes, Jonny, you do.

I wrapped myself up within the hotel's grey bricks, I was safe in the isolation, safe from the storm that was both battering the landscape and also raging inside of my head. Would I be at this place now if I'd not ended up nearly dying in Cornwall? Would I have noticed how incompatible Paul and I have become if I'd not been in so much danger? Of course, the danger now is that no one else will ever measure up to Jonny. I trace the outline of his face on the paper. How could they? How could they ever be as amazing as him?

I knock the drink back and the barman looks at me curiously. I give a half shrug. "Can I have another please?"

"Sure."

He rinses the cocktail shaker and I turn my attention back to the picture. It doesn't do Jonny justice really, despite the obvious talent of the photographer. It doesn't show the contours of his face or the stubble that has the smattering of grey, nor the topaz flecks in his silver wolf eyes that I found myself lost in over and over. It's him in all his rugged beauty, but there is none of the charisma in the photo that makes Jonny so spectacular. Damn it. I should throw the picture away and forget I ever met him.

The barman places my drink down and I give him a smile. "Thank you."

"I've made it a little stronger, you look like you need it!"

"You have no idea." I mutter, folding the paper and putting it back in my bag. "I'd better have my bill too please."

He presses a few buttons, and a slip of paper comes out of the small printer to the left of the till. I take it from him and rummage in my bag for my purse. He lays the card machine on the bar and I tap. So that's it, no more hiding. I down my drink in one. It's time to go home.

✳✳✳

Paul is in the kitchen when I walk in through the door. He looks me up and down and bursts out laughing. "What the fuck are you wearing."

"Hello to you too." I mutter, pulling the chords either side of the hood to tighten it around my face. It smells of Jonny, the delicious citrusy scent that filled every room he was in.

"Why are you sniffing that hoodie, you weirdo!"

I want to cry. I feel tears prickle behind my eyes so I clench my hands into fits and will the tears to go away.

"Honestly, Molly, you look like a bag lady." He opens his arms in a grand gesture. "Come here!"

I don't want to, but my legs stiffly walk me the few steps into his arms. He wraps them around me, but it feels wrong. His body feels different, and he doesn't smell right. It's a more synthetic scent, rather than the musky, masculine scent that Jonny had. I shouldn't compare them, it's wrong. I'm wrong. I should have gone straight to Ella's.

"I missed you." Paul's voice doesn't sound right either, he's trying too hard. It makes me feel as though he's covering something up.

"Did you?" Not enough to warn me about the storm though.

"Yes, I've been horny all week." Nice.

"Would you jump with me?" I ask him. His arms loosen slightly before he pulls me in closer.

"Huh?"

"I nearly died, and I'm scared of water now, would you jump with me?"

"Sounds like you've watched Titanic one too many times, Moll." Paul laughs, letting go and standing back.

"But would you?"

"I'm pretty sure once you've had a hot bath and you're in your own clothes, and had a good nights' sleep, you'll be able to jump into water with no worries."

"So, you wouldn't then?"

"I'm not Leonardo Di-sodding-Caprio, Moll." He laughs to take the edge off his words and glances at his watch. "No time for a quickie now, Jake will be here in a minute. Lot's to tell you though, been an exciting week. Shame your course didn't happen though. I got a refund, so I'll treat you to The

Spa instead. Gutted, I was thinking I'd have decent food for life."

I nod mutely.

"You're being really fucking strange, Moll." There's a horn toot from outside. "I'll see you later. Have a bath or something, some wine…whatever it takes to make you normal!"

I nod again. *Say it, Molly, tell him it's over.* Instead, he pecks my cheek, grabs his wallet, phone and keys from the worktop and walks out the door. I feel nothing.

I hear the car drive away and then burst into tears. The mound of birthday presents are still on the floor where I left them on Saturday. I should be itching to open them, instead they feel like the reason of all this angst. I pick up my phone and find the number.

"Hi Molly," the cheery voice answers.

"Ella, can you come over?"

"Now?"

"Yes."

"Are you ok?"

"No."

"I'm on my way." Ella hangs up the call and I chuck my phone on the counter and walk into the lounge. It's all *me* in here. My choice of paint colours, accessories, my photos, my pictures. There is nothing that says Paul even lives here, apart from the games console attached to the TV. Even the photos of us are in frames I chose. As I walk around our tiny flat, I cannot see 'us' anywhere. I push open our bedroom door. It was tidy when I left but Paul has left dirty clothes and laundry strewn over the floor, the bed is unmade with the sheets in a tangle in the middle of the mattress. I suddenly wonder if he's not been here alone. I sniff the air.

It smells sweet in here but as I've been living with damp for four days it could always smell sweet. I sniff again. Then like a crazy person I start smelling the sheets. What am I hoping for? To find out that Paul has been cheating on me while I've been away as though it will take my guilt away? Would it make the decision to leave him easier if he had someone else to go to? Would it make me feel better? I sit down on the bed and hug a pillow to me. Then I cry. Great sobs rip through me, and tears fight for space on my cheeks. Perhaps it's all just post-trauma and I'll be alright in a few days but Jonny's face flashes up in front of my eyes and his voice rings in my ears and I know that I will be anything other than alright.

Jonny

"How the fuck is this shithole going to be ready for Saturday?"

"It's not." I sigh as Chelsea slams her cup down on the coffee table. She's been slamming things all day in her usual dramatic way. It doesn't matter how many times she asks, or how angry she gets or how many doors she bangs against walls, my answer is the same. It's exhausting. She is exhausting. In the bright light of day, the hotel looks infinitely worse than I'd imagined and there is no way we'll be opening for months and months. Everything needs ripping out and replacing but at least I'm covered. Thank fuck for the person with the sense enough to arrange the insurance. They need a pay rise, because if it had been left to me, we'd be totally in the shit. Even more than we are now. The letters from GameNeekz are in a box in the corner of the bar, but with Chelsea here, opening them will have to wait. Chelsea picks up the vape from the coffee table and inhales.

"That's bad for your health." I say, coughing as she blows the smoke at me.

"You're bad for my fucking health."

I sigh and close my eyes. I wish Molly was here. I wish we were still trapped by the storm and laughing over something silly. I wish I'd not let her go, even though I had to. She's too good for someone like me to shit all over, but I miss her and it's an ache that hurts as much as losing my music. Everything feels empty without her.

"So you keep telling me."

She snaps. "I hate you, Jonny, I fucking hate you. You've ruined my fucking life. How can I show my face in town again? Everyone is supposed to be coming. Everyone. Do you know what that means?" She doesn't wait for me to answer. "It means that I look like a twat. It's alright for you,

you don't have any friends, but all mine are coming, and I promised them a huge fucking party with champagne and fireworks and now there is no fucking party. I don't know why I married you. It was the biggest mistake of my fucking life." Chelsea stops her rant and bursts into angry tears. I don't try to console her, there's nothing to say. I don't plan on saying sorry for the party, I didn't want it anyway. But I did ruin her life and I am sorry about that.

"Chels..."

"Don't talk to me. I hate you."

"You don't really."

"I do." She wipes her eyes. "I really do. This isn't how I thought it would be."

"It's not how I thought it would be either." I lean forward on my chair and reach for her hands. The red nails shine in my palms. "I think we should face up to the truth, Chelsea. We are wrong for each other. Our marriage just makes us miserable and that doesn't feel like the right way to live our lives. You deserve more than that, and hopefully I do too. None of this is your fault, Chels, it's all on me. I did this to us. I'm so sorry that I took you down with me."

Chelsea takes a shuddering breath in and she suddenly looks so young. Under the thick makeup and surgery, she is still in there somewhere, the beautiful girl who blew me away. I wish I could have given her the life she craved but the universe had other ideas and it wasn't meant to be. We were incompatible from the beginning. It was the sex and my arrogance that made it happen. Chelsea should have just been another woman I fucked and forgot. It would have been kinder to her. *Remember whose son you are, boy.*

"You're right." She says eventually, ripping her hands from mine. "It is all your fucking fault. You are a loser and a has-been, and I am going to take you for everything. Even this fucking shit pile. I'm having the lot."

16

"Chelsea," I say softly, "you can have more than you think, but not this hotel." There is too much of Molly here to give the hotel up. "I will make sure you have enough and that you are looked after. This life isn't the one you signed up for, I won't let it affect your future…"

"You keep saying there is no money," she sniffs. "How can you give me what you don't have?"

"There is an investment I've recently found out about." I stop short of telling her about the castle. There is something about it that makes me want to keep it secret. "I don't know what it means financially, but it will mean that there is some money. And what there is, you can have a share of."

"A share?"

"I don't know how much the investment is worth yet." I wish to fuck I'd not said anything and just left it all to the lawyers to sort out.

"You have money and you've not told me? I've been stressing over my credit card limit and you have money?" She shrieks, her tone like nails down a blackboard.

"I didn't know I had it until two days ago, and I don't even know how much it is. I'll be transparent, Chelsea, you'll get money. I won't see you short."

"No, you fucking won't." She snaps and drags on the vape. "There has to be something good to come out of this shit show, Jonny and you don't have to worry, you can keep this cesspit. I don't plan on ever coming back here again."

I smile gently and she glares at me. "I'm sorry I wasn't what you wanted me to be."

She takes another drag and blows out great plumes of smoke. "You were everything once. Everything I wanted, but then you fucked it up, and I have no idea why." She shakes her head slowly, "it's ok, I survived all of that and managed to have a great life anyway, not here obviously, because here sucked. I have fabulous friends so it's fine, I suppose, but I'll tell you this, Jonny, I can't be poor, not like

17

before. I won't go back to that life and end up knackered and old like my mum." Chelsea shudders. "I left all that behind so if you don't do right by me, I'll sue you for everything." She looks so young and scared that my heart twists. I remember her life before. The poverty she lived in, and the siblings that she had to care for while her mum worked three different jobs. We sorted her mum out in the end, but the weight of living under the cloud of never having enough has taken a toll.

"I know."

She stands up and puts the vape into her bag. "Shall I get a lawyer?"

"It would be a good idea."

"And the money?"

"I will get all the figures to the accountant and the lawyers can work it all out. You'll be ok, Chels, I won't let anything bad happen."

"It already has," she says sadly. "I thought I had married a rock star and instead..."

"I know, you got me."

"There is nothing here of mine, so I'll just go."

"Ok."

She smiles softly and for a moment she looks like she did when we first met. "I hope you will be alright down here all alone."

"Why? Are you offering to stay?"

"Fuck no!" Chelsea puts on her coat and walks towards the door. "I want to be sad but I'm not sure I am."

"There isn't anything to be sad about."

"No, there isn't." Without a goodbye, Chelsea walks out of my life.

✳✳✳

I make a coffee and take it through to the bar. Now that I'm alone it's time to go through the letters from GameNeekz. My heart picks up its pace as I lift the box up onto the coffee table. I didn't lie to Chelsea, I will see her right, but I don't know what that means. This is a strange situation, to have an investment I knew nothing about but, I laugh to myself, the strange situation seems to be one that I repeat over and over – the investment, the hotel, the castle! It's not what normal people do but it always seems to happen to me. I turn up the radio and open the first letter.

Dear Mr Raven
We have been trying to reach you to advise you of monetary payments due from the investment you made in GameNeekz in nineteen-ninety-five. As of the date of this letter you are entitled to a sum of £500,030. Please contact us so that we can arrange payment of monies due.
Yours faithfully
D Fields.
Accountant for GameNeekz

Half a million payout for a hundred grand investment? I was savvier than I gave myself credit for! I reach for the next letter, dated a year later.

Dear Mr Raven
Further to my letter dated 1st October 1997, I write to advise that we are now wishing to pay you an additional sum of £1,004,000. Please do ring my office so that I can arrange a transfer of funds.
Yours faithfully
D Fields.
Accountant for GameNeekz

One million? Holy fuck. I open the next letter dated a few years later.

Dear Mr Raven
I note that you have not yet responded to my previous letters, so I sincerely hope that they are reaching you. My clients have had a successful launch of a new game and the profits include payments to you. The sum that I have in trust for you is now at £3,700,045 which includes previous amounts that I have been unable to transfer to you. Please do call my office at your earliest convenience so that I can arrange payment.
Yours faithfully
D Fields.
Accountant for GameNeekz

Each letter contains more and more notices of payments due and when I finally add them all up, the investment has gained me eight million pounds. Eight million! The miserable life that I've been living should never have happened. How the fuck did my accountant not know about this? The castle I can understand, it's in my old name, but he can't even find the ten million I hid to avoid paying it to my first wife, Melanie. What the fuck am I paying him for?

I pick up my mobile and punch in D Field's number. A breezy woman picks up and gives a greeting. When I say my name she immediately transfers my call. I listen to the tinny hold music until the line gets answered.

"Mr Raven?"

"Mr Fields?" I reply.

"I was beginning to think you didn't exist."

"I didn't," I say lightly. "My apologies for all your correspondence being unanswered, I've not been on top of my admin."

"I hope you have managed to now read all my letters?" He asks. He speaks with a tone that I remember from school. A patronising tone my teachers used when they wanted to tell me that I'd amount to nothing.

"Yes, I have, and that's why I'm ringing. I understand you have money in trust for me?"

"I do, indeed." I hear him tapping away on a computer. "I have the sum of eight million and forty two pounds to transfer to you."

"Great, shall I give you my bank details."

"Actually, Mr Raven, you need to come to my office. I cannot pay this without proof that you are who you say you are."

"How many Jonny Raven's have you been trying to contact, Mr Fields?"

"With all due respect, Mr Raven, you could be anyone. Shall we say midday on Monday?"

"Where are you?"

"In London." He sounds surprised I asked. "If you have a pen I shall give you the new address, it differs to the correspondence I've sent you."

He rattles off the address that I scrawl onto the back of an envelope and ends the call. Eight million quid. Fuck. A trip to London for the first time in half a decade, bigger fuck. London feels like the big bad after so long. It chewed me up and spat me out when my career came crashing down. Damn it, Jonny, life is ever complicated. I chuck the letters back into the box and drink the coffee, before leaving the bar and heading to the pool. A swim is what I need to clear my head, because otherwise I will give into the whispers of the whisky bottle, and I still bear the scars of the last time.

The corridor smells of stagnant water but thankfully the huge arched windows have survived the storm. Most of the building survived, with the exception of the conservatory and the front door, which is still held in place by the desk until someone can come and refit it. I push the spa door open and strip off my clothes, jumping into the cold water. *I'll jump with you. I've got you.* God, I miss the little waif who washed up at my door. I miss her so much that it has become a physical pain from which there is no escape. I need her with me and it's unnerving because I've never needed anyone. *Molly isn't just anyone though, is she Jonny?* No, she is The One.

Molly

"OMG you're not serious?" Ella slops red wine onto the floor as she stares wide eyed at me. "I know exactly who you're talking about. Do you remember when I dated Ben and he was into all the rock stars, and I became a rock chick for a couple of months..."

"I think I have erased that from my memory!" I laugh. "Ben was not one of your finest moments!"

"No, he wasn't but the music was. I drove my parents nuts with all the base and smashing drums that I played as loud as I possibly could. I probably did it on purpose, to be fair! Anyway, Jonny Raven was his idol. He was so handsome, all broody rock star with the growly voice and those eyes...I used to dream about his eyes! Ben even bought contact lenses to try and look like him! Did he have those eyes in real life? I can't believe you were with him. I would have sold my soul...Do you know how cool this makes you?"

"If only," I mutter, "I would be happy with cool..."

Ella puts her glass down. "Oh, honey," she says softly, "you look so sad."

"I feel so sad." A lone tear rolls down my cheek. "I feel heartbroken. It's irrational and ridiculous but I do. I was only there for three days so these feelings make absolutely no sense."

"Love doesn't make any sense," she says taking hold of my hand. "It's not supposed to, if it did none of us would ever feel anything for anyone. Maybe you were meant to meet him to know that things with Paul have just got worse and worse? I mean, I always liked Paul, he was a bit, you know, vain and narcissistic, but a pretty good guy overall but I can see that something's changed and he's not the same as he was, Moll. Since you started your business, he just puts you down all the time. It's like he's jealous because you're so fabulous and he's so not. Even Robbie has noticed, and he doesn't notice anything."

"Your boyfriend isn't the most observant of people, is he?"

"Never, so if he's noticed..."

"So, what do I do, El? Where do I go? I can't afford the rent here alone, but I've looked at other available flats in Bath and they are so expensive that I don't think I've got an option other than to move out of the city. I suppose I could get a lodger but I don't want some weirdo, and what if Paul won't move out? What do I do then? I can't stay here with him because that would be no good for either of us."

"You can stay with us!"

"I know, and that's lovely of you but I can't sleep on the sofa bed in your lounge indefinitely and you need your space. It won't be very cosy if I'm there all the time."

"We'd manage, Moll but if you didn't want to then could you go to your parents?"

"God, no! I love my parents, but last time I stayed at theirs, my dad told me off for drinking and expected me to go to bed at nine! He still thinks I'm fourteen!"

Ella laughs. "Yeah, I couldn't go home either." Her face falls. "You need to tell Paul, Molly. He has to know that it's over and he can stay with one of his scrot friends if you don't want to stay on our crappy sofa bed. Is there no way you could stay here?"

"I can for a while, a month or two, maybe. The rent has just been paid and I've got some savings but they won't last long if I have to pay for everything by myself."

"I can help if you get stuck. I got a bonus from work..."

"I can't take your bonus." I say.

"You can as a loan. It's going towards our deposit but we're way off having enough, so you can use it for now. I think moving out of here would be too much upheaval, and, in any case, why should you be the one to move out?"

"Because I cheated."

"It was one kiss, Molly, not an affair."

"My heart cheated."

"Wow, Moll, that's dramatic, even for you!" Ella laughs and I giggle.

"I know!" I sigh and look down at the glass in my hand. "Trouble is, Ella, I don't think I'm ever going to be the same again. I feel..." I pause to find the words, "let down, rejected, abandoned. Paul not caring enough to let me know that the course was cancelled was the wake up call I needed but then Jonny didn't want me Ella, even though I was so sure he did. His kiss was...God, it was perfect. I've never had a kiss like it, so soft and gentle and filled with meaning. There was no way it was just me that felt the feels, but then he said some shit and told me to go so now I don't know what to do. I was sure I survived the near-drowning because I was meant to meet him, but how could that be right when he didn't want me." My voice goes up an octave as the pain in my stomach tightens its grip. "He didn't want me. He jumped with me and there were so many signals...I'm an idiot, such an idiot." The tears spill over and Ella takes my glass and, putting it on the table, wraps her arms around me letting me cry.

"You don't know what your future holds, my lovely friend, but you deserve the world."

"The world is shitting on me..."

Ella shakes her head, "it just feels that way. You've had a really traumatic experience and your relationship is in the toilet so it's going to seem like the universe is conspiring against you, but it's not. There is a lesson in this, and it's to put yourself first. Forget Paul, he's not your forever and you can't stay with him because Jonny said no..."

"I wasn't planning on staying." I interject, "not in a million years."

"Good. Let's look at the positives. Between us we have enough for your rent and bills for the next couple of months which will give you some breathing space then you can decide what you're going to do. Paul and you are over so that gives you the freedom to get to know yourself again."

"What would I do without you?" I ask, wiping my face.

"The same as if I had to do without you, fall apart!" Ella grins, "boys we can live without, but each other, that would be the reason for admission to the asylum! Take the moment, Molls, ring him and tell him to come home, I'll go." She says, knocking back her wine, "I can pop down and see Georgie, then I'll come back when he's gone."

"How did I get here?" The tears fall again, "everything was so simple and now it's all wrong. So, so wrong. I have a knot in my stomach that is suffocating me, and I flick between bawling my eyes out and savage rage in a nanosecond. It doesn't help that I probably have some form of post-trauma shit from nearly dying, which Paul doesn't think was a big deal, but the worst part is that I feel like such an bloody idiot. All I can think about is Jonny and wondering if he is missing me like I miss him, but then I want to give myself a slap for being so bloody wet. I'm not wet, I've never been wet, so why now?"

"Because you fell in love, and it's knocked you off your path. It's no wonder you feel discombobulated, four days ago you had a different life. Us humans like things to stay the same, there is safety in knowing. The minute something changes, we feel completely overwhelmed and struggle to function properly until the new becomes the old and we feel safe again. Then another change comes and so on…It's how life works, but it can still knock us. Molly, you're being way too hard on yourself. Paul is a prick. Why the fuck he thought a catering course would be good for you, I'll never know. He just stopped thinking. He is all about him, and you were someone who slotted neatly into the World of Paul and now you don't want to slot in anymore. I get that. And it's a good thing. It's been a long time coming. As for Jonny, why are you so certain he doesn't feel anything for you?"

"He told me to go, Ella," I mumble.

"Yes, but he also said he hurts people and he wasn't going to hurt you. That is what you say to someone you're crazy about, but past experience is making you cautious."

My hand shakes as I lift the wine glass to my lips. "I wish it was that simple," I say and knock the contents back in one. "I wish I never met him."

"No, you don't!" Ella laughs.

"No, you're right," I fill our glasses up to the brim. "I don't."

***

Paul slams the door and comes into our small lounge. My cheeks are tight where the tears have dried and I feel deathly cold despite still being wrapped up in Jonny's hoodie. I should take it off really, but there is comfort in it, proof that he was real, that I didn't dream it, even if I find myself questioning everything. Paul looks cross, a frown marring his handsome face.

"What's so important that you called me back?" He demands, swaying a little in the doorway.

I look down at my hands which are balled into fists and I long to slam them into Paul's flushed face. When did he start speaking to me with such distain? More to the point, how long have I allowed it for. Is Ella right, did I just slot into the World of Paul and play the role of a dutiful girlfriend? Has he always put me down? I thought I was stronger than that. A photo on the window sill catches my eye. I remember the moment. It was a trip to London that he surprised me with when I got a promotion at work. When was it? Five years ago? Less? More? I can't remember when we last had a trip like that, where we laughed and laughed and were so together that I didn't think anything could break us apart. The face now glaring at me is a stranger, no longer recognisable as the one smiling in the photo. I sit up a little taller.

"I need to speak to you."

"Couldn't it wait?"

"No." I say sharply, "no it can't wait." I stand up. "I can't do this anymore, Paul. I can't live like this and more importantly, I don't want to. I need so much more than what we have."

"What the fuck? You dragged me home to moan at me?" He slurs. "Seriously? Honestly, Molly. You're such a *girl*."

His face reddens and I suddenly feel angry. "I'll take that as a compliment because being a girl is so much more awesome than a dick like you would ever know. So, yes Paul, I *dragged* you back because what I have to say couldn't wait."

"Oh, just get on with it will you." He says, reading a text on his phone. "Simon's waiting in the cab for me."

"Let him fucking wait. I couldn't give a shit. I have had enough of you dictating to me, I don't know how I ended up like this but I've had it with everything. This relationship is over, Paul, because it's not good for me. You are not good for me. I am sick of your endless picking and moaning. You make out that everything is my fault, but the reality is that you're jealous..."

"I'm what?"

"You heard me."

"Why the fuck would I be jealous of you?" Paul hisses. "Are you drunk or something?"

"No, I'm very, very sober." I tuck my hands inside of the hoodie sleeves and take a deep breath. "Even if I was hammered, the fact remains that I don't want to be in this toxic relationship. I don't think you want to be with me either, because if you did, you would not treat me the way you do."

"Are you accusing me of treating you badly?" He shrieks. "Me? After everything I've done for you... you're so fucking selfish Molly."

"Am I? Selfish? When you're the one who left me in a storm that nearly killed me because you were more interested in being on the lash!"

"You're not still going on about that, are you?"

"I won't ever forget it. It was the most terrifying moment of my life, Paul. I don't think you realise how serious it was. I nearly fucking drowned. There was a tidal wave and it tipped the car over and I could have died. This isn't some overdramatising of a rainstorm, it was real. You were hungover after a night of drinking with your mates, while I was fighting to stay alive." I pause. Paul doesn't say anything which surprises me. "But it's fine, Paul. Really, it's fine, I learned a lot about myself in the past few days and I know that moving on is the right thing to do."

"So, that's it, is it? You've decided so that's it, I don't get a say?"

"Yes, pretty much."

"You're moving out then?"

"No. I don't have anywhere to go, Paul, and at least three of your friends have spare rooms. I didn't ever imagine..."

"Well, fuck me..." Anger erupts from Paul, "What a bitch you are! I buy you an amazing gift that was really fucking expensive and all you do is moan about it, making me look like a twat for bothering and now you want me to move out. After all the support I've given you..."

"Support?" I say astounded. "When have you supported me?"

"When you got made redundant, I sent you so many jobs..."

"I didn't want those jobs."

"No, you didn't because you think you're a goddamn interior designer! I mean, what the fuck Molly? I gave you time and let you dabble in that shit because I'm a fucking great boyfriend, and instead of being grateful, you dump me?"

"You *let* me dabble? You let me? Have you heard yourself? What gives you the right to take my achievements away from me. I don't dabble, I work really bloody hard."

"No, you don't. You paint some shit and show off about it."

"Show off?" I screech longing to throw the nearest heavy item at his head, "is that what you think? That all I do all day is show off? I was going to take a share of the responsibility for our relationship failing but you are just a total prick. Admit it, you hate my job because you are jealous that I've made something more of myself and wasn't going to settle for the boring work I was doing before. My business stopped you having any control and that's why you bought me a cooking course, because you hate everything I've achieved."

Paul splutters, turning a worrying shade of puce. "Because it's bullshit, Molly. You got lucky, that's all, you have no talent, no experience, no business model, you just got lucky."

"Did I? Lucky? My clients wouldn't agree with you and as they're the ones who pay me, I think I'll trust their judgement." I shake my head. "I thought I'd feel sad at the ending of our relationship after all these years, Paul, but I don't. I feel nothing but relief, and that is truly heart-breaking. It's over Paul and I want you to move out. Tonight."

"What the fuck…"

I sit down hard on the sofa. "It's not entirely your fault, Paul, despite what I said." I say softly, "I am just as much to blame. We shouldn't be ending this way, with all this bad feeling. We should be ending because we are holding each other back. I can't be the person you want me to be, and you aren't the person that I need. I don't want someone trying to walk in front of me, I want someone to walk alongside me, being proud, supporting me, listening when I speak, and you can't do that." He tries to speak but I hold up my hands, "and it's ok, Paul. It's ok. There will someone else for you who loves everything you have to offer, and you deserve that, like I deserve more." I rub my eyes and rest my head on my hand, elbow on the arm of the sofa. "I know it's difficult but I'd like you to move out because I don't have anywhere else to go. I think that's fair…"

"Do you." Paul says sharply, his words slightly slurred. "You think it's fair to make me move out tonight, when this is the first I've heard of it?"

"No, it's probably not but…"

"Probably not?" He says with a coldness to his voice. "I'd say definitely fucking not."

"Paul," I say firmly, "I know this has come as shock, but I have to put myself first for once." I shrug, "no one else is going to, so it's up to me. Whether you like it, or not, whether it's fair or not, whether you're angry or not, it's just how it is. I am breaking up with you and nothing is going to change that decision."

"I don't give a shit, Molly. I don't want to change your decision, in fact I feel fucking relieved that I don't have to listen to your moaning anymore. It will be interesting to watch you try to afford the rent on your little hobby?" I glance at him. He looks menacing and nothing like the person that I've spent so long with. I suddenly feel fearful.

"What the fuck is taking you so long, mate?" Paul's friend Simon comes barging in. "The missus giving you earache again?"

Simon is a dick.

"She's only chucking me out of my own fucking house."

I don't bother to respond.

Simon says, "fuck her mate, get your toothbrush and let's go back out. Jake has got the beers in and that bird you were speaking to wants to know if you're going back. If she -"

Simon gestures at me, "-doesn't want you then fuck it, you're in with whatsit in the pub, so let's go."

Paul pushes past me to the tiny bathroom and gets his toothbrush, shoving it into his back pocket. "Fuck this shit." He says, and leaves the flat, slamming the door behind him.

I sink lower onto the sofa and pull my knees up to my chest, wrapping my arms around them. I couldn't have handled that worse if I'd tried. I feel a strange sort of sadness, the end of an era I suppose. Paul will be ok, he has some *bird* who will make him feel less aggrieved, but that's it for me. No Paul, no Jonny and eventually no flat. Shit.

I unwrap my legs and shift to reach for my phone. Selecting a number, I wait for it to be answered. "Ella, he's gone."

"I'm coming." She says kindly.

I hang up the call and promptly burst into tears. So that's it. Where do I go from here?

Jonny

"Jonny Raven, it's been too long." My lawyer, Jim Hartell opens the door and grins at me. "I thought you'd died."

"I did."

He laughs, "I'm glad to see that's not true. You look well, Jonny, better than the last time I saw you."

"Last time I was probably hammered, it was a daily reality..." I shrug, "it's been a while since I've had a drink." Four weeks, three days and ten hours, but who's counting.

Jim nods, "that's good to hear! You look better for it."

"Wish I felt it!"

"Coffee then?" I nod once. Jim looks at his secretary, "two coffees then, please Rose," and ushers me into his office. I've not been here in years, not since the final property got sold but it still looks exactly the same. I clock the spirits on the small dresser to the right. Once upon a time I'd have helped myself, drunk the lot and then sent him a case of whiskey in the post. Today coffee will do just fine.

"So, what do I owe this honour?" He asks, sitting in the huge leather chair at his desk. I sit in the small one opposite.

"I find myself in the strange place of having money again."

"Good..."

"And, a wife I need to divorce."

"Ah, a wife and money doesn't often go well. I'd have thought you'd know that by now, how many wives have I arranged settlements for?"

"Two, this is my third, and last! It's not much money, eight million..."

"Eight million? What did you do? Rob a bank?"

I laugh, "nothing as exciting. An investment I didn't know about came good. I thought Chelsea could have three mill, is that reasonable?"

"Under what terms are you divorcing her? Adultery? I've seen the photos..."

I give him a scathing look. "Unreconcilable differences or some shit like that. No one is in the wrong, I just want out of the marriage."

"It may cost you more than three million."

"I have a hotel to completely redo after some major storm damage, she can't have more." I sigh. "I want her to be ok, Jim, it's not her fault." He gives me a look that I ignore. "She can't take me for everything because I need some of that money and also make sure that I can continue to support Aria and her mum. It has to be a watertight agreement because I want to protect any future earnings. I can't imagine I had a prenup?" Jim shakes his head and I shrug. "Ah well, she may just accept the offer with no fight because there is no blame, it just didn't work out."

"Does she have a lawyer?"

"Yes," I lean over and scribble a name on the pad sitting on the desk. "I will cover the costs."

"Anything you're keeping from me?" Jim asks eyeing me. "No missing millions that have been uncovered, no palace anywhere?"

I don't quite meet his gaze. "Missing millions, yes and when I find them, you'll know. Definitely no palace." A castle, but no palace.

"I'll get the paperwork drawn up." Jim leans back in his chair. "it's good to see you mate, Cornwall is obviously suiting you, you look well."

"Do I?"

"Yeah and sober too, that helps! So, tell me, when can we expect new music?"

"Why? Are you looking at a new condo in the sun?"

"Always!" Jim laughs, "I heard one of your songs on the radio the other day and," he shrugs, "it was pretty good."

"Pretty good?" I grin, "you wouldn't know good music if it hit you in the face!" Molly's face swims into view, and her laugh when she sang along with the boy band. The pain of missing her hasn't gotten any easier with the passing weeks. "There's one more thing, Jim. I want you to arrange the anonymous purchase of this property and have the deeds drawn up in this name."

Jim looks at the paper I hand him. He scrunches up his forehead. "Why?"

"Just because. Can you arrange it? Without my name being involved?"

"Is it rented?"

"I believe so."

"Then yes, I can arrange it. How much are you prepared to spend?"

"As much as it takes."

Jim laughs, "are we looking at wife number four?"

"No," I shake my head slowly, "I would never do that to her! Keep it quiet, though Jim, no one is to know. I have your word?"

"You do. It must be serious, who is she?"

"She's the woman who saved my life."

**

London hasn't changed much in the past five years. The same smell, the same heavy atmosphere, the same manic rushing around. Everyone still avoids eye contact and pretends no one else exists. I can't remember the last time I sat on the tube, but as there are still limited funds in my bank account it's the cheapest way for me to get around. I suppose I can understand why Chelsea likes it here – the pace and the opportunities for her make London the centre of the universe but for some reason, it just makes me feel claustrophobic, old and slow. Isolation has changed the way I live my life, mostly for the worst, but since Molly landed on my doorstep my view of Cornwall has become something more. I want the hotel to be its best self, I want to make money, I want to live with my head held high, I want my words back and to feel the rhythm in my soul again. I want to forget I ended up in a big, black hole and make something of the rest of my life. I want Aria to feel the same pride in me as I do in her and, one day, I want to see Molly again. When I'm good enough, when I'm not likely to drag her down.

I check the tube map. The office of the GameNeekz accountant is a short walk from Tottenham Court Road so I change trains at Leicester Square and wait for my exit. The woman sitting opposite me has a copy of the magazine in her hand and her eyes narrow in recognition as she looks from it to me. Shit. It's still being sold? I give her a half smile that she returns.

"Can you sign this?" She asks, "I was a huge fan." She corrects herself, "I am a huge fan."

"Sure." She rummages in her bag for a pen.

"I'm Cassie. Can you sign it to Cassie?"

"Yes, of course."

"Is it true?"

"Is what true?" I take the magazine and the pen from her and scrawl her name and mine on the inside page. I know what she's going to ask, and I brace myself for it.

"What they said? That you're not coming back? No more music?"

"I'm not sure yet. There hasn't been the right song…"

"It must be sort of right then, if you're on the tube? Surely you'd have a driver otherwise?"

"I like the tube." The lie hangs in the air as I hand back the magazine and the pen. "Don't believe everything you read." Except it's true, all of it. There isn't any music and there isn't likely to be. Perhaps if I hadn't have told Molly to go, there may have been. Who the fuck knows. The train slows into Tottenham Court Road and I stand up. "Nice to meet you, Cassie."

"You too." She smiles at me and flicks through the magazine to the page I've signed. "Thanks," she gestures with the magazine, "at least my colleagues will believe that I met you on the train!"

I leave the train and stuff my hands into my pockets and join the crowd moving towards the escalator. Damn it, being recognised was not part of today's plan, or any day. I can hear the conversation now, *guess who I saw on the tube? The tube! You'll never believe it, I was reading an article about him and there he was. On the tube! It must be true! He is poor!*

I cross the road and walk up a side street to the address on the letter. It's a non-descript black door set between two coffee shops with a buzzer for entry. I push it and wait for the response.

"Arderton Fields can I help you?"

"It's Jonny Raven to see David Fields."

"Come on up, first floor." The door buzzes and I push it.

I suddenly feel nervous. Knowing there is eight million quid waiting to be collected is making breathing difficult. Once it would have been a small, insignificant amount but now it's life changing. It's a refurbished hotel and my daughter's education, maybe even her first home. It's Chelsea's future but mostly it's my peace. That's what I want. Peace and quiet, away from the voices, time to just find out who I am, find the beat again. It's space. Fuck, it's everything all rolled into one cheque.

"Mr Raven? David is waiting for you." A pretty receptionist greets me at the top of the stairs. "You found us ok, so many get lost."

"Yeah, pretty straightforward." She's trying not to size me up, keeping her features neutral but her eyes can't disguise her thoughts. I smile and she flushes. *I know what you're thinking lady!*

She coughs. "This way please." I follow her along a short corridor, trying not to look at her curvy arse. Once I would have taken her into the nearest stationary cupboard and banged her, which is what she clearly wants judging by the sassy walk, but not today. Not tomorrow either. Fuck knows when. Maybe a good fuck is what I need to take my mind off Molly. I can't remember the last time Chelsea and I were in the same room long enough. Forty-five years old and I may as well be impotent.

"Mr Raven, I presume?" A bald man in a too-small shirt comes out of the office in front of us.

"That's me!"

"David Fields. Delighted. Huge fan." Yeah, right. "Coffee?"

"No thanks, I've just had one, water would be good though."

"Lauren, can you get Mr Raven a glass of water. I'll have a coffee." He steps backwards into his office, "come in, come in." His office is full of more shit than mine but somehow he manages to locate a file from under a pile. "Take a seat, Mr Raven, and let's look at your financials. Did you bring your ID?" I nod. "Good, good. So we've been trying to pay you for a number of years, but you've proved to be elusive, part of the job I suppose. I have here a transaction to approve for eight million and forty-two pounds. Can I see your ID?" I take my wallet from my back pocket and hand over my driving license. He studies it and then my face, "and where would you like this money paid?"

"Into the bank…"

"Obviously, which one?"

"You're going to do it now?" I ask incredulously.

"That's the joy of everything being online," was he trying to be funny? "I can just do it."

"Eight million quid, just like that?"

"You are who you say you are, no reason for me to hang onto it any longer. Unless you want a cheque?" He laughed. "You know, Mr Raven, it's never been so hard to give someone their money, ever. I think you're the record!"

"It wasn't intentional, I assure you, and Mr Fields, I am well aware that everything is online these days. I just assumed it was more complicated than a quick transaction."

"Not anymore!" David Fields types on his laptop and then says, "do you have your bank details?"

I pull up the details and hand him the phone. He presses a few more keys. "All done. Eight million and forty-two pounds will be in your account within two hours. Hopefully it won't take so long to pay you the next dividend. We look to pay every six months, but now I have your account details I shall just pay you and send you the certificate."

"Nice one," I say, "thanks."

"Any idea what you're going to spend it on?"

"Finding some peace." I say standing up, "thanks."

"I hope you find it!" David stands up and holds out his hand. I try not to look at the damp patches under his arms, darkening the shirt.

"Yeah," I reply taking his offered hand and giving it a firm shake, "me too."

***

I take a cab back to my budget hotel and check out. The eight million is in my account almost immediately so I take another cab to The Stark Hotel on Park Lane. It was the setting for many a debauched night, more cocaine, whiskey and women than I could ever count, but somehow it feels like coming home. I remember it. I remember the laughter and the raucous behaviour. I remember how nothing was ever too much trouble for the staff who ran around making sure I had everything I wanted. Half of them I took to bed, and then forgot about when I sobered up. I remember the early days, when everything was on tap, what I wanted I got, who I wanted to fuck, I fucked. I didn't give a shit about anything other than getting my own way. John Jones was buried under a ton of excess and it nearly killed me in the process.

Three rehabs, maybe four, organised by Freddie, who bundled me out of this hotel, and plenty of others, paid off women to keep them quiet, out of sex clubs where I snorted cocaine from naked breasts, and bars where I drank so much I barely knew my own name – a lifetime ago. The drugs stopped but the drink and women, there was no end to that. Twenty-two years of hedonism and then nothing.

The cab pulls up to the hotel and the driver gets out to lift my suitcase from the boot. I pay him and acknowledge the doorman as I walk into the hotel. It's changed. Or maybe I have. I drop my case by the reception desk and ask for a room. I'm shown to one that looks out over Hyde Park. It's nice. It will do. Then I close the curtains, fall onto the bed and sleep.

Molly

"I don't understand." I look from the smart man wearing a suit, to Ella and back again. "The flat is mine? How? When? Huh?"

He looks exasperated and Ella giggles behind me. "Basically Moll," she says slowly, "someone, and one guess as to who, bought this flat for you."

"Just like that?"

"It seems so!"

"Mine? Not Paul's?"

Ella takes the document from my hand and looks at the front page. "According to this it's all yours."

"Well...fuck!"

"Quite!" The man mutters. "If you would kindly sign this, Miss Bloom, I can leave you in peace."

I sign the document confirming receipt of the papers.

"Thank you," he says. "Congratulations on your home." He turns quickly and walks back to the car idling on the road.

I close the door. "The flat is mine?"

"Oh my God, Molly!" Ella laughs, "for someone so bright you really are being completely dumb!"

"I don't understand."

"Isn't it obvious? Your Cornish star-crossed lover bought it for you."

"Jonny? No way!"

"Who else would? Paul hasn't even come back for his stuff, unless he has done this because he's thinking you'll cool down and have him back. I suppose that could be feasible if he had the cash stored away. But he's been a dick so..."

I take the document from her hands and curl up on the sofa to read them again. It doesn't make any sense but it's there in black and white. I own my flat. I try to come up with a logical explanation but can't find one other than Ella's. Did Jonny do this? Really? *You found him millions, you found a castle and over the past few weeks you've been following a trail...maybe he just wants to say thanks.*

"This is bullshit." I suddenly snap making Ella spill her wine. "Bullshit. There is no way this is Jonny, no way. He didn't want me, why the fuck would he buy my flat? And," my voice goes up an octave, "why wouldn't my landlord have told me the flat was being sold? Aren't they supposed to give notice on shit like that?"

"Your landlord probably didn't even think about it, because you're already in the flat. He would have had to say something if someone else was moving in. Does this mean we can dump all of Paul's stuff into black bags on the step?"

"No, Ella, we can't do that."

"Shame."

"He's not that bad! He was a good boyfriend..."

"Until he wasn't! I still haven't forgiven him for buying you a cooking course. I mean, for fucks sake who buys that for people under the age of fifty?"

"Yeah, but that course changed my life."

Ella shakes her head, "maybe," she says softly, "but regardless of that, you are still sad. Whether it made you open your eyes to how things had changed with Paul, or not, you are still sad." She kneels down in front of me and takes my hands in her warm ones. "You've got thin, love, and you look tired. You've been working like a maniac. Your spark has gone and you were so alive before. Go to him, Molly, if he is the one for you, then go to him. Don't sit in your flat and be grateful he bought it for you, go to him. Make him see sense. It sounds like you meant as much to him, as he did to you."

"Hardly! He told me to go."

"It's a love story, Moll, they always have to have some drama, otherwise where is the fun?"

"I don't want drama," I mutter, "I want...oh, I don't bloody know what I want." The document is heavy in my hand. It makes no sense. The flat is mine. My name is on the deeds with no mortgage, rent or anything owing. Mine in full. An anonymous purchase. A gift. I want to feel elated but I feel flat. It's the ultimate goodbye.

"Moll?"

I can't speak to her. I suddenly feel exhausted. She's right, I've been drowning in work so I don't have to think or feel. I've not seen Paul. He hasn't replied to any messages and he's not been for his stuff. Maybe what Ella said is true, maybe he's just been waiting for me to calm down and then he'll come back. We've fallen out before, once at uni, the silence lasted a month until we found our way back to each other and then that was it. Decision made. We were a couple. But this time, my decision is final and I don't want to be with him. I'm hoping he left here with Simon and found someone else - he's handsome, charming and was a good boyfriend for a long time. I want him to be happy because, despite my grumblings over the past couple of years, and the way I ended our relationship, I do care about him.

"I feel like this is the ending of the end." I flap the deeds, "something like, thanks for hanging out with me, thanks for finding some money, here's your flat and have a nice life."

"When did you become such a negative ninny?" Ella asks sharply, "honestly Molly, right now I think you need a slap. Wake up! This is huge. Huge! This isn't the ending of the bloody end! This is the beginning of the rest of your life. You have your own home, that you love, and you don't have to worry about paying for it because someone felt so much for you that they gifted it to you. I mean, what more do you actually want?"

"Jonny."

"Molly," she says, "you know me, I love drama and the will-they-won't-they but as much as I wish this was a tv show and that it will all end up perfectly, this is probably all he can do. You said he's been to hell and stayed there, maybe this is everything he is able to give of himself. It speaks volumes but you're not hearing any of it. Stop feeling sorry for yourself and let's go out!" Ella tops up my glass of wine. I don't want it.

"I don't want to go out."

"I don't give a shit, you have to stop this now, you're being ridiculous." Ella says crossly. "You're acting like it's the end of the world, and it's not. I don't want to be *that* friend but fuck me, Molly, you're not a teenager pining for a boy, so stop bloody moping. It's giving you wrinkles! I think it's obvious that he has feelings for you because he's made sure that you're ok. It's proof that you had something, even if it can't be anything other than one kiss. Honestly, Molly, just stop it and get in the shower, we're going out..."

"Ella…"

"Don't you say anything else, Molly Bloom! We are in our prime, we should be out in town, dancing and celebrating your flat, your singledom and anything else we can think of! Now either go and have a shower or I'll drag you into the garden and hose you down, one or the other!" Ella looks fierce and I start to laugh.

"You're so right." I pull a face, "what's happened to me?"

"Change happened. It can make a person feel completely all over the place. A few drinks and a good dance and you'll be right as rain. You'll get your spark back, Molly, you just need a cocktail!"

Wearily I drag myself up and walk towards the bathroom. Ella is right. This isn't me. I'm not a moaning, miserable person but since I've got home from Cornwall I've ended up in a slump and I don't recognise myself. Everything has changed, all in one go, but she's spot on, change isn't a bad thing. Not at all. This is the beginning of the rest of my life. I turn the shower on and stand under it, letting the water wash everything away. No more dwelling. I can't hang on for someone who didn't want me, regardless of the generous gift of my home. I'm not a marriage wrecker and I'm not a cheater. I take some grounding breaths and then finish my shower, getting dressed into the sparkliest dress I own and adding bright makeup to my pale face.

"That's better!" Ella says approvingly and goes off to raid my wardrobe for something she can wear.

My laptop blinks but I ignore it, whatever has just come through can wait. I'm following a trail to Jonny's missing money which has given me something to do in the middle of the night when I can't sleep. The path is getting clearer but I'm not sure what I'll do when I reach the destination. Ring him and say, 'hi Jonny, remember me. I've found your money, congratulations you're rich again, your wife will be happy. Have a nice life.'

"Molly?"

"I'm ready, let's do this! Bath, watch out!" I laugh.

✷✷✷

The hangover is something from the depths of hell. I roll over and brace myself for the stabbing pain to shoot through my head. I lost count of how many drinks or how many shots and I have no idea how I got home. There is movement in the lounge and a dramatic groan followed by retching. Ella must have stayed the night. The world swims and nausea rises from the pit of my stomach as I slowly sit up. I'm not slow enough because my stomach cramps and my mouth is flooded with acidic saliva. Oh God, I'm going to be sick. I reach for the bin just in time and a flash of memory hits me like a bullet. Jonny rubbing my back as I vomit into his bin, warm soft hands, silver wolf eyes, dazzling smile... Fuck off Jonny, I'm trying to forget you.

"Moll?" The door opens slightly. "Are you awake?"

"I don't know." I croak. "I think I've died."

"I've died too. I can't stop being sick and now my insides hurt." She flops down on the bed and grimaces. "Jeez, Molly it stinks in here. Something is decomposing."

"It's probably me decomposing and that smell is vomit. Whatever we drank has poisoned me." I lean over the edge of the bed to throw up in the bin again. My tongue sticks to the top of my mouth as I speak, "what the fuck did we drink?"

"I don't know!" Ella moans, "I haven't felt this rough in ages. Oh my God, Molly, I am never, ever sympathy drinking with you again."

"I'm never giving you reason to," I say, "if this is what miserable ends up feeling like, I'm giving it up. Jeez, what a state to get in. You'd think we'd have learned by now that we never go drinking to forget a man."

"Do you remember the night we had when I'd broken up with Ben? We raided my mum's martini? I thought I'd died then too." Ella turns a vile shade of green, "urgh, pass me the bin."

I shove the bin at her and hold back her hair as she throws up again. "Never again, Molly. I swear to God, next time you have to handle your shit yourself, I'm too old. I'm having flashbacks to tequila. How much of that did we drink?"

"I don't remember drinking tequila."

"Well, we did, and I bloody hate tequila. It's the stuff of nightmares. I don't want to be awake anymore, Molly, everything hurts." Ella pulls a pillow down from the top of my bed and puts it under her head. "I'm just going to have a nap."

"Like that? You're hanging off the bed!"

"I can't move," she mumbles and closes her eyes. "I'm going to stay here for a little moment, until the room stops spinning. Ok?"

I crawl back up the bed and lie across it. "Ok." I whisper, finding a cool spot on the pillow to put my head on. "I think I will sleep too."

"Night Moll."

I'm too hungover to point out that it's mid-morning. It's too much effort to speak. "Night Els," and with that, I drift off to sleep.

Jonny

"It's not great news, Jonny." Jim Hartell says when I answer his call. "Chelsea has agreed to the three million you've offered but she also wants fifty percent of the music royalties and half of all the profits you made from the start of your relationship until the date the degree nisi is served."

"Fifty percent?" I splutter and drop the phone. Fuck me, is she having a laugh. "You're joking, right?"

"Nope." I hear rustling of papers and then Jim says, "Her lawyer has stated that due to the decline of her mental wellbeing and spousal neglect, her rights to the monetary value of the marriage is justified. She believes that she was a good wife, and fulfilled her vows but you didn't, and therefore she is entitled to the lifestyle that she expected at the time of your marriage."

"Is she including the birthday concert?" My heart sinks. That show made a fortune in tv rights, merchandise and music sales. "Because, if she is, then there won't be enough money for that. Can you fight it?"

"Yes, of course. We can fight everything. We can use her expenditure to counteract that, use her social media as evidence. Rose is saving images now. Looking at the details your accountant sent over, it seems that she spent considerably more than fifty percent of the joint income but contributed nothing. It could get bitter, Jonny, you need to be aware of that."

"I'm too tired for bitter." I say, picking up the mug of coffee. "Offer her an extra five hundred thousand, but that's the lot. There isn't anything else to pay her from anyway."

"The hotel?"

"It's currently worth nothing because of the storm damage and no, she can't have that. In the past five years she's been to the hotel a handful of times. She hated it, hated Cornwall so no, that property is off the table! Besides, the renovations are going to cost a fortune and she'll end up having to pay the three million back!"

Jim laughs. "I'll get onto the accountant, and we'll send back an amended offer. I still, to this day, don't know why you married her."

I do. I know exactly why I married her. It was so no one else could have her. I thought she was the perfect woman, the divine mix of slutty and sweet. I married her because I was obsessed with her and she was equally obsessed with me. I was her meal ticket out of poverty and she was the deliciously sexy woman that everyone wanted to fuck. It was never going to work because love didn't come into it. It was mutually beneficial and despite her protestations that she loved me, I know that she never did, and I didn't love her. I've never been in love, until Molly came along.

"It's one of life's great mysteries," I say lightly. "Did the deed transfer go to plan?"

"Yes, all delivered."

"Good." I feel relief. At least Molly will know. She'll know that she meant something even if I did let her go. It was the right thing for her. I would have messed everything up and ruined her life, like I did to everyone who has ever been involved with me. *How do you know*? I just know.

"I suggest you organise some way of pausing royalty payments to prevent having to give Chelsea any additional funds..."

"There aren't any!"

"I keep hearing your music on the radio, Jonny, there will be more than you think. That miserable article has got everyone talking, according to my teenager, you're the GOAT!"

"I'm the what?"

"The Greatest Of All Time, it's kids speak!" Jim laughs, "you need to be careful, Jonny. You may end up making more money than ever, for doing absolutely nothing. Isn't it about time you started singing again, now that all the kids like you, it's a brand-new audience to wow."

"Wow? I don't think I remember how to wow!"

"Then you need to remember it and fast, before the next old-but-new singer comes along. Haven't you heard? The eighties are back because of some tv show! It won't be long before we're back in illuminous socks and shell suits!"

"I was a little kid in the eighties, but if shell suits excite you then go for it!" I laugh, "I'm not sure if I'll ever sing again, but good to know that I'm a goat!"

Jim chuckles, "ok, *goat*, my next appointment has just arrived, I'll be in touch." He hangs up with a brief goodbye. I put my phone down on the bar table and finish the coffee. Then I surprise myself. I turn the music up until my ears ring. It's cheesy pop, the sort of shit Molly would listen to and the pain that hits me takes my breath away. I miss her. I miss everything about her - the laughter, the terrible jokes, her smile and kindness, I miss how I felt when I was with her, how she saved me... I miss her so much and I never thought I would ever feel such an all-consuming need for another person ever. I vowed I wouldn't. I watched how my dad broke my mum over and over again, until she couldn't take another beating, but she went back to him, after ten years of safety. She said it was love, but I didn't understand how love could be made from all that violence. So, I didn't love. There was no fucking way that I was going to be anything like my dad, beating the shit out of someone and then, while they cleaned up their wounds, telling them that it was because I loved them so much. I was never going to love. Apart from Aria who I was smitten with from the moment she came into the world, purple, screaming and covered in gunk.

Then my song comes on the radio, and I'm not prepared for it. My first worldwide number one, the record that put me on the map and changed my whole life. My voice booms out of the speakers and I'm momentarily paralyzed. That was me.

50

Once. I remember being him. A superstar with everything I wanted, and more. I had so much material crap it was fucking disgusting. Just a click of my fingers, a casual slip of my name – and every excess came on a silver platter. It's a wonder I'm still alive.

I want to turn the radio off. I want to rip the speakers from the walls and sit in the blackness but I don't move. If I move, I'll hit the whiskey, and that's a road I don't need to go down again. I nearly drowned. If Molly hadn't been washed up on my doorstep, I would have given up and waited for the whiskey to claim me. It's calling me now. Taunting me from across the bar. It would be so easy. I'm not sure I'd even be missed. How fucking sad is that? Perhaps Aria would for a while, and maybe Molly would. Fuck…I can't think about her because if I do, I'll sink. Losing her has been my greatest ever mistake.

I reach for the phone and dial Jim's office number. When the receptionist answers I say, "it's Jonny. Can you get Jim to ring me the minute he's out of his appointment? There is something I want him to do."

***

"Let me get this straight," Jim chokes and coughs to clear his voice. "You want me to sign over power of attorney to a woman you've known for three days? Have you lost your bloody mind, Jonny?"

"Not at all." I grin, feeling a little gutted this is a call not a face to face. I'd love to see his expression.

"Are you drunk?"

I laugh, "no, I'm not drunk. I'm sober, of sound mind…"

"There's nothing sound about your mind." Jim says sharply, "do you have any idea what you are asking? You could lose everything. Everything, Jonny! You've just started making money again and now you're handing it all on a plate for some woman you don't know. You're mad. Mad!"

"I'm not handing everything, just the hotel and all decisions relating to it. Insurance, redecoration, anything that's needed. The hotel is covered so almost everything can be paid for by the insurer, and what isn't covered then Molly can use the money she has access to. I want you to deal with Tom Masters, my accountant, about the money, and a salary for Molly. You handle all the legal stuff. I'm going away so I'll come and sign anything you need for her to have access to the building before I go. The power of attorney can be revoked when it's all done. I don't want to be involved. You can leave it all to her."

"Have you spoken to Freddie about all this? He usually deals with..."

"Freddie and I have parted ways." I'm sure he says, *I'm not surprised.* "Can you do this?"

"Yes, I can, but as your lawyer I have to advise against it..."

"I don't need advice, Jim, I just need it arranged. I want Molly to oversee the refurb, that's it. There is nothing else to discuss. I'll come to London the day after tomorrow with the keys, the alarm codes and the insurance documents. I expect you to pass them on to her."

"And there is nothing I can say to change your mind?"

"Nope."

"I think of all the insane things you've done over the years, Jonny, this has to be the most insane." It's not, but he doesn't need to know that. "Fine," Jim continues, "I'll get the documents drawn up. Usually, the person who is taking power of attorney needs to be involved but I can bypass that, somehow. What are you going to do?"

"I am going to figure shit out."

"Oh."

52

I look down at the print out of train tickets. "I'm not sure 'oh' quite covers it. Thanks, Jim, I'll see you in a couple of days." I cancel the call and chuck the paper onto the table, trying not to consider what would happen if Molly said no. I wasn't going to have her do the refurb, wanting to protect her from me in as many ways as possible, but there isn't anyone else I trust to do it right. How fucking sad is that? I'm forty-five and I have no one. Not one fucking person to have my back. All the awards, record sales, *yes* people and I have no one at all. *You have Molly.* No, I don't because I pushed her away and besides, she was never mine to have, not really. Even though she wanted me to ask her stay. Fuck, why didn't I? Why didn't I just take the chance that I wouldn't fuck it up. *You know why.* I hope she knows how I feel about her, which she may if she's realised the flat was a gift from me, but part of me hopes she never thinks of me again. *No you don't.* A wild, guttural roar erupts out of my mouth and I slam my fists down on the table, knocking the coffee mug over. I let it spill, watching the black liquid drip onto the carpet, with no mind to clear it up. "What's the fucking point," I mutter.

Above the silence, the whiskey bottle on the bar whispers my name, over and over until I can't take it anymore. I head to the swimming pool, dropping my clothes as I walk along the corridor, before jumping into the cold water. It makes me gasp but I pound my way up and down the pool until all my mind can do is focus on the strokes. I don't want to think, because if I think I'll go to her, and she doesn't need this version of me. This fucked up, broken version of me. If I'm going to fight for Molly, then I have to fix it. I have to fix it all. And, the only way to do that is get as far away from people as I possibly can.

Molly

"What the fuck are you playing at?" Paul storms into the flat and throws his keys down onto the worktop. "I was staying away, giving you space and you fucking screw me over..." He waves a letter from our landlord at me. I was planning on telling him, once I knew how to say it, but it seems the landlord didn't worry himself about word choices.

"I didn't screw you over."

He looks mad. His face is red and his eyes flash with a fury I've never seen before. He rakes his hands through his hair before slamming his fist down on the counter. I wonder if he wishes that it was me he was slamming his fist into.

"You fucking did, Molly, and you know it. You come back after what you *claim* is a traumatic time, dump me, make me move out and then, poof," he gestures wildly with the letter, "as if by magic, the flat is yours, even though I know you can't have earned enough to buy it, doing the shit you do. You're taking me for a fucking idiot, Molly. Who bought this flat for you? Because shit like this doesn't just happen. Who the fuck is he?"

"There isn't anyone." My lie rings in the air and I try to arrange my face to look innocent, but he knows I'm lying.

Paul narrows his eyes and glares. "At least have the decency to be straight with me Molly. I can forgive you, if you tell me the truth. Just be honest. I'm honest with you." The shifty look that creeps across his face tells a different story. "I've tried to help you even though you've been weird for months, and I've apologised for the Cornwall stuff...what more do you want? I'm sleeping in Simon's spare room on a single bed that I keep falling out of when all I want is to be back here, in our home, with you. Like it always has been."

"I don't want that, Paul." I say, balling my hands up inside the cuffs of Jonny's hoodie. "What we had isn't enough anymore. It's no one's fault, it's just that things changed. I changed." It isn't anyone's fault, not really. I want to blame Paul for it, but I'm self-aware enough to know that I gave him all the power and that's on me. "I need more than what we had, and right now I just need to be alone. I have to figure out what I want and what my future holds. I can't keep being second in a relationship, I need to be equal."

"So what? You're now first because you've somehow got the flat? You broke us up just to win?"

"No, of course not. That's not what I meant..."

"It fucking sounded like it."

"Maybe it did." I reach for his hand. "You're a good man, Paul. You were a good boyfriend, and you will make someone happy, but we're not right anymore. We haven't been for a long time, and if you're honest, you don't want this, not really."

He sighs loudly and draws his hand back. "You're right, Molly. I don't want this. It's been shit since you got made redundant and I can't carry you anymore, I can't pretend that your hobby is something special. I hate to say it Molly, but I don't even fancy you these days. I've tried but you're such a mess all the time. I can't remember the last time I saw you when you weren't covered in paint or wearing shit like that." He waves his hand up and down at my choice of hoodie and joggers. "You used to be sexy but now you look a fucking state. Ah well, at least I tried. I'll take my stuff and that will be it. I'll be gone and when you realise you can't live on your..." he gestures speech marks, "new business, don't come running to me because I won't be there to bail you out. You're on your own, unless of course, your new man will."

"There isn't a new man."

"Don't give me that. You can't afford this place..."

"How do you know?" I snap. "How do you know I can't?" He's right. There is no way I could have ever afforded the flat on my earnings. My business is good but not good enough to buy a two bedroomed flat in the centre of

Bath. "You know nothing about my business and I'm glad about that. It used to really upset me that you were so blasé about what I achieved but now, I don't give two shits what you think, or what you know. I thought we could be civil to each other after all these years, but you obviously don't want that, so we're done. Done, done, done. You need to move your things out, I don't want them here."

"I'll collect them tomorrow. No need for you to be here. I'll leave the key." Paul gets up and crosses the room to the door. "I'm fucking glad I didn't waste a few grand on a ring, the cooking course was too expensive as it was…"

"The cooking course changed my life, Paul, I'll always be grateful that you gave it to me."

"Screw you, Molly, screw you."

He slams the door behind him. I pull up the hood of Jonny's jumper, and watch him walk down the short path, letting the tears roll. After all these weeks, the hoodie no longer smells of Jonny, but it makes me feel comforted to be wearing it regardless. I didn't expect to have such overwhelming sadness at the finality of Paul and I ending, but I suppose after so many years it would be strange if I didn't. The once clear future is now a total unknown and I have to have faith that the universe knows where I'm going. Until it all becomes clear I just have to keep working on my business and keep pushing forward although right now, I could murder a drink.

I pick up my phone and select a number. "Ella?" I say when she answers, "fancy a drink?"

"I'll be right there."

Faith and a drink. Here goes nothing.

***

"Miss Bloom?" The friendly voice at the end of the phone is at odds with the hangover from two bottles of cheap red

wine that Ella brought over. *It's all the corner shop had,*
she'd said. I'm not surprised, it tasted like out-of-date
vinegar. But, we drank it anyway and now the bright light
flooding the lounge and the chirpy lady on the phone are like
hammers on my already pounding head. The drinking has to
stop.

"Yes," I reply thickly. I wonder if she notices.

"I am calling from the law firm of Hartell and Caine, on
behalf of Mr Jonny Raven."

My headache is forgotten. The sudden painful hammering
of my heart bashing against my ribs makes me feel sicker than
the hangover I was experiencing. "Has something happened
to Jonny?" I croak, bracing myself for the worst possible
news.

The woman pauses and then gives a tinkly laugh. I want to
punch her. "Oh no, Miss Bloom, I'm not phoning for
anything like that."

"Oh thank God." I slide down the wall and sit heavily on
the floor, the glass of water in my hand spilling as I sink. "I
thought for a moment…never mind, how can I help you?"

She rattles off information at breakneck speed and my sore
head doesn't keep up. "I'm sorry, you're going to have to
repeat all of that." I say contritely, "I'm not firing on all
cylinders today."

"In a nutshell, Miss Bloom, Mr Hartell would like to meet
with you in London at your earliest convenience to discuss a
contract to complete the renovations on Mr Raven's hotel,
following the extensive storm damage. There are documents
you need to sign if you are willing to take on the work,
monies to agree to, management of accounts and so on…it's
all quite straightforward."

"Jonny wants me to do the hotel?" I didn't imagine that
the hotel refurb would still be mine. I assumed he would have
chosen someone with considerably more experience than me,
despite him saying otherwise at the time. I don't want to

regress and become the analytical teenager, pouring over every word a boy says, but it's hard not to. Surely it has to mean something? Surely? It's too big a deal not to, isn't it? I get lost in the ping pong game of thoughts going back and forth - yes it does! No it doesn't, he's just making good on his promise! Yes it does! No it doesn't, he's just making good on his promise, on and on until I realise the woman is speaking to me.

"Miss Bloom?"

"I'm so sorry, this has been a lot to take in and I'm a little shocked."

She mutters something that I'm glad I can't quite hear. "When are you available to come to London?"

"Ummm, hang on, let me check my diary." Damn it, I have two big furniture projects to complete. "Would the end of next week suit?" My inner voice is yelling at me to fuck the furniture and get on a train today.

"Friday next?"

"Yes, midday?"

"Perfect. If you let me have your email address, I'll send you confirmation and our address."

I tell her and she thanks me, cancelling the call and leaving me staring at the phone in shock.

Refurbishing the hotel? Oh. My. God. When my brain cooperates I ring Ella. "Els, you'll never believe what's happened now."

***

"Well, Molly, I think it's safe to assume that your long-lost love is definitely feeling all the feels for you. You must be one hell of a kisser!" Ella says, grinning up at the waitress who brings our coffee and breakfast. "I'm tempted to find out myself."

"Oh jog on, you idiot!" I laugh and thank the waitress who looks at us with interest. "It is mad though, to think that I have a twenty-bedroomed hotel to do, with no other input. It's all on me. He must feel really bad."

"Nah," she says, adding sugar to her coffee. "There's no way anyone would take the risk on a new designer just because they feel bad. I'm telling you Molly, he's got the feels!"

"Where did you get that bloody expression from?" I ask.

"I'm addicted to Love, Life and London, it's all about the feels." Ella laughs and I throw a sachet of sugar at her.

"Perhaps become unaddicted."

"Oh, stop it, you know full well that you've been wondering what it all means!"

"Yeah, maybe a little." Ella raises her eyebrows and I admit it. "Ok, a lot, but I also feel very confused by it all. What with Paul and now this, I swear my brain is going to melt!"

"Forget Paul, he's just a prick..."

"No, he's not a prick." I shake my head, "I gave him too much power and ultimately, he just wasn't right for me. Imagine if Robbie went away for a few days and came back completely changed."

"As long as he came back with the ability to pick up his own pants, I wouldn't mind!" Ella laughs and I giggle. "You can't take all the blame for it ending though Molly, half the time he didn't treat you as well as he should have."

I grin, "Paul is blaming it all on me."

"Of course he is. He's hardly going to blame himself, is he?" Ella bites into her toast. "God, I needed this, my hangover is so bad that all I can think about is carbs. So much for getting into my bikini in a month."

"You brought shit wine."

"You needed a drink."

"Yeah, I did!" My hand shakes as I reach for my coffee. "The trouble is that the endless drinking is just making everything feel all the more confusing. God knows how I'm going to focus on painting furniture when I am thinking of nothing but how crazy my life has become."

Ella liberally adds jam to her second slice of toast. "I'm not surprised you're feeling confused. There are mixed messages flying everywhere. Paul being all '*take me back,*' then '*fuck off Molly*' and Jonny with his '*I can't be with you, but can you do my hotel, oh, and here's the deeds to your flat.*' I'd be lying in a dark room with a cold compress and IV of gin if I was you. You're holding things together pretty well, all things considered."

"I'm not so sure! I feel like a fucking teenager." I grumble. "Do you remember the endless nights trying to decode boy stuff? I thought the days of game playing were behind us!"

"Oh my God, if you think that then you're insane! The game playing is what keeps life interesting, and the endless battle to be top banana…"

"Top banana? Is that another expression from that show?"

"Yes, and I like it, stop judging…the passion comes from the game, Molly. Taking it in turns to be top banana, or alpha, or whatever word you want to use. It's also about letting the other be top, then you then them…although on top has always been my favourite."

I laugh, "seriously Ella!"

She raises her eyebrows and grins, "the trouble with you and Paul is that he hated it when it was your turn to be top banana. He hated it so much that all he did was put you down, as though belittling you would make you less fabulous. That's why your relationship broke, it was nothing to do with you having your own business, it was because you were really bloody successful at it, and then you became more successful

60

than him so his ego cracked and that's when it all went wrong."

"That's what I told Jonny…"

"There you go." Ella leans back in her chair with her coffee cup nestled in her hands. "So, you know."

"Yes, I do know. But if a relationship is balanced on the game of top banana, how did Paul and I last so long, because I was never top banana."

"Because you allowed him to always be, so if anything happened to him you would know you gave him your all."

"Do you think that's because of what happened to Corey?"

"Yes, the trauma from a situation like that is monumental. Hell, I'm still trying to get over it and I was just the girlfriend's best friend. You were the girlfriend. Paul was your get-over-trauma boyfriend, Moll. It was the relationship that was supposed to show you what you don't want only it lasted years longer than it should have."

"I told Jonny about Corey." I say and wipe away the single tear that rolls down my cheek. "There was no *you should be over it now, Molly,* or *are you still on about that Molly,* just kindness and understanding. Why do I have to have to two people that I miss so much? Isn't one enough?"

Ella reaches across of my hand. "Everything will work out for you, my gorgeous friend, and you will have all the happiness you deserve. Sometimes there are lessons to be learned in the darkness and once you learn them, the sun shines again. If you and Jonny are meant to be, you'll find each other."

"You need to stop watching rom-coms."

"You just need to trust me, Molly, I am far wiser than you know!"

I laugh, "if you say so, Els, if you say so."

"I do say, but maybe not today! Today my head just hurts. You're a terrible influence on me!"

"I'll buy the breakfast as an apology."

"Toast and coffee? What am I? A cheap date?"

"If the shoe fits, Ella…"

"Cow!"

Jonny

"Are you sure I can't change your mind?" Jim asks handing me paperwork. "This is a terrible risk. You're literally signing over the hotel to a woman you don't know. What if she isn't who you think she is? I really must advise you against this, Jonny."

Tom Masters nods his head. I'm wishing I'd not asked my accountant to come to the meeting. "I'm in complete agreement with Jim." Of course, he is. "This is insanity Jonny, you've only just got your bank account looking healthy, and now you're risking it all on a complete stranger."

I grin. "Gentlemen, I appreciate your concern for my mental and financial wellbeing, but I can assure you this is absolutely what I want to do. I'm not handing over the deeds to the hotel, I'm handing over security codes and the legal rights to act on my behalf with the insurers and renovators. I'm not saying *here you go, chick, take the lot.* I need to keep money away from Chelsea who seems to be after every last penny and Molly is the way to protect that cash. If she has it for property works, even temporarily, then Chelsea can't get at it."

"No, Chelsea can't, but this woman can. She can have three million quid in her bank account and spend the lot. You'd have no way of protecting it." Tom says looking at me as though I've lost my mind.

"Molly will protect it." I lean forward and rest my hands on the desk. "I've trusted her with my deepest, darkest secrets and I can trust her with my money. If I'm wrong, then I'm no worse off than before..."

"How can you be so blasé about money?" Tom asks, "you've been moaning for years that you've not got any and now you're signing it all away. You must be mad, or drunk, Jonny. Sane people don't do this. Sane people invest their money and enjoy the rewards."

"I am investing it. I'm investing it into the hotel, you should be proud of me. The old me would have just pissed it up the wall."

"I think I preferred the old you." Tom mutters, "and why the sudden urge to do up the hotel. I would have thought you'd want to do the bare minimum then sell it."

"I did once, but I see it differently now. It's a money maker, and besides, the insurance is paying for most of it, I just don't want Chelsea to know that! Anyway, what's with all the opinions, I don't pay either of you for opinions..."

"No but we invariably end up having to sort out all the shit."

"That's why you're the best, Tom!" I flash him a beaming smile, "sorting out my shit is your talent."

He sighs, "what am I signing over to her then?"

"This is-" I pull a folded piece of A4 paper from my pocket. "-where I want money to go. I'll leave the battle with Chelsea to you two, but she can only have what I've got. Jim, you can work your magic on the divorce settlement, but as far as I'm concerned, she can't have any more than I'm offering. Be ruthless if you have to be because it's three point five mill or nothing."

Tom takes the paper. "A trust for Aria, yes, I can arrange that. A payment to Susie, ok. Money to this Molly woman, I think you're crazy but if that's what you want then fine, and," he squints at the paper, "is that all you're giving yourself?"

"What do I need money for? I have no life!" I grin, "stop looking so worried Tom!"

"It's what you pay me to look like!"

"Well," I say, leaning back in my chair and crossing one leg over the other, "if my plan works, I'll be able to pay for you to have Botox!"

Jim laughs, "ever the optimist."

"It's my new outlook!" I grin, "at least, that's what I'm trying to convince myself."

***

I walk back from Jim's office to the hotel and take the route through Hyde Park. The sun is high in the sky, where it's been sitting since the day Molly left Cornwall. At times if feels as though I'm being taunted by the weather, but the bright blue is preferable to being in a musty, damp and damaged building in Cornwall on my own. I get a sharp pang in my chest when I realise that I'm asking Molly to do just that - be alone in a musty, damp and damaged building. I haven't even considered her safety, nor how she would feel about being in the place where she nearly died, without anyone to support her through any trauma that she is still holding onto. *It's also the place that you rejected her.* Fuck, I know. I know that, and it makes it all worse. I am an arsehole for asking her to do it but it's the only way to tell her how I feel, without telling her how I feel. She probably hates me anyway, regardless of the gestures.

I stop at a coffee cart to buy a drink and a bagel, sitting on a bench near the lake. Even for a week day, it's busy. There are runners, skaters, mums pushing buggies, exercise classes dotted around the park. Life carries on. I am in an isolated bubble of...I don't know – anguish, upset, fear? – a mixture of all of it probably, but life is still doing its thing, the world is still turning and I am still here. By the grace of God.

"Let's sit here," a woman says to her friend, pushing a brake on the pram with her foot.

Her friend hands her one of the two coffee cups and they sit on the bench next to me.

"Do you remember when I was obsessed with that rock star?" The first one says. "Jonny Raven."

I shrug down inside my coat and pull the cap lower on my head.

"How could I forget." The friend laughs as she puts the cup to her mouth. "I thought Dave was going to leave you."

"It was a close call! I had to promise to take the picture out of the downstairs loo or he would make me go to couples counselling!" She giggles, "he forgets he has a crush the size of Texas on that Australian actress, the one who took her clothes off and showed the world what she had for breakfast! I can 't remember her name, but you know who I mean! Anyway, I was listening to the radio on Saturday morning and Jonny Raven's song came on and it was like I was twenty again. You should have seen me clambering into the loft for all my CDs. Dave was like, *have you gone mad, woman,* but I told him that it was true love then and it's true love again now!"

"So couples counselling is in your future then?"

"Probably. I'd forgotten all about Jonny Raven, he just disappeared. Then yesterday morning I was getting Sophia ready for nursery, half watching one of those nostalgic pop programmes and his video came on. I was so engrossed that Sophia ended up at nursery wearing only one shoe!"

"You're such a teenager!" Her friend laughs loudly.

"I know, but it gets worse! Last night I had a major sex dream about him, and now I can't get him out of my head."

I grin to myself and wonder if I should stop by them and say hello, but my ego wants to hear more.

"You are so sad," her friend laughs, "honestly, I don't know how Dave puts up with you."

"I don't either but because of my rampant sex dream about Jonny Raven, Dave got a morning shag that he will never forget, and he actually whistled as he left the house!"

I snigger and throw my empty coffee cup into the bin. I can't help myself as I stand and walk past, "the question is, was I any good?"

She glances up and me and drops her coffee as recognition floods her face. "Fuck."

"Apparently we did," I grin and hold out my hand, "Jonny Raven, pleased to meet you."

Her friend stares opened mouthed at me.

The woman looks mortified. "Did you just hear…"

"Every word," I say watching her flush even deeper. "I'm glad I was of service!"

"Oh my God." She buries her face in her hands. "Oh my God! I'm so embarrassed."

Her friend laughs, "she'll dine out on this forever, you realise that!"

I grin, "it's a hard job, but someone has to do it! Enjoy your day, ladies!"

"Wait!" The woman lifts her hands from her face, "can I get a selfie? Or an autograph, or something so I know I'm not dreaming!"

"If you were dreaming, we'd probably be doing it against that tree. Twice!"

Her friend laughs louder, "Dave is going to get the ride of his life after this!"

"Shut up, Candice!" She says, standing up and smoothing her hair. Taking her phone from her pocket she looks at me. "I can't believe you heard what I said!"

"My ego is very flattered!" I put my arm around her shoulder and pull her towards me, "say cheese!"

Her friend takes a number of photos and hands the phone back to her. "I think you've just guaranteed her husband gets a morning shag until the end of time!"

I laugh and drop a kiss on the woman's cheek. "Have a good day." I say and walk away from them, listening to the squeals as she looks through the photos. "Well, Jonny," I muse, "you've still got it!"

"Hey Dad."

"Hey kid, what you up to?" I'm sprawled on my bed at The Stark Hotel, watching a movie that I've not been paying any attention to. I keep thinking about the woman in the park yesterday and what that has done to my ego. I feel validated. I'm annoyed about it, but it's the truth.

"Not much, heading to hockey practice in a minute," Aria says cheerfully, "we've got a derby match on Wednesday, and we lost last time, so coach is making us practice every single minute! I'm pooped! So, where are you, Dad?"

"I'm in London..."

"London? Not with idiot Chelsea?"

"No..."

"Good, because she was on Instagram yesterday literally snogging someone, it was gross. She is gross..."

"You know it's all over Aria, I told you."

"I know, and it's great but I had to check." She takes a sharp intake of breath, "I mean, sorry if you're sad about it, Dad, but...well, I'm not sorry. I think it's a good thing."

"It is a good thing. We were not right for each other."

"No, you really weren't, and at least now I don't have the shame of her being my step mum. I can't tell you how much Bitchy Bonnie went on about it, every single day 'oooh look Aria, look at your stepmother, look what's she's doing'...It was so embarrassing. Everyone followed her because they thought she was cool, and I wanted to shout, 'No she's not cool, she's a...' never mind. Sorry if you're sad."

"I'm not, I'm fine."

"Good!" She says brightly, "but I'm choosing the next girlfriend, Dad, you always pick idiots!"

"That's rude, Aria." I say sharply. She's right, though. I do. Always the pretty ones, the sexy ones, the enticing ones, the ones that everyone else wants, the challenges, the ones who intrigue me, at least until I get them into bed, then they are discarded onto the scrap heap. I wonder what Aria would think of Molly who isn't an idiot, just kind and open and generous and so, so, so pretty.

"Sorry Dad, but you're only cross because you know I'm right!" She laughs, "anyway, I've got a date."

"A date? A date with who?"

"It's *whom*, and his name is Jett."

"They let you out of school for dates? At fifteen?" Fuck me, fifteen-year-old boys are all hormones and no sense and they're hanging out with my daughter. Fuck that.

"We have weekly events with the boys' school down the road. You can't lock up a load of teenagers in single sex boarding schools and expect them to be socially responsible adults, Dad!"

"How do I not know any of this? Does your mother know?" I feel outraged. I also feel guilty. I've had weekly phone calls with Aria for years and I don't think I ever listened. Always drunk, always thinking about being drunk...what a despot father. Just like my own. *Don't forget whose son you are, boy.*

"Of course she knows! Seriously Dad, it's not the dark ages! We have events on Saturdays, and we can go to town on Sundays. We have a curfew so it's not like I stay out all night and bonk behind a bush..." ⃞⃞⃞⃞⃞

"Do not even think about bonking. Ever." I splutter, sitting upright on the bed. "I mean it, Aria, teenage boys can't be trusted."

"Chill Dad, it's a date. The first date! He's nice, you'd like him!"

If anything is going to drive me back to drink, it's my daughter on a date. I make a coughing noise that sounds like 'bullshit.'

"Honestly, Dad, you need to do some yoga or something and breathe! He's nice, I wouldn't go out with someone who wasn't. I am more sensible than you know." She sighs, "I've got to go now, I need to get to hockey. Enjoy London, see

69

you at half term, love you." She hangs up before I can return the sentiment.

I shift off the bed and stand in front of the long windows that look out over Park Lane. I'm not ready for my daughter to be making decisions about boys. How is she even old enough to be going on dates? When did it happen? I've missed so much of her life because even now I still think of her as being little, chubby-cheeked with a mass of auburn hair and the cutest laugh. How her laugh used to fill me with such joy. Then life went dark for me, and I've missed it all. She grew up while I was a drunken waste of space, bitter over a lost career and existing on whiskey and regrets.

"Fuck it." I mutter.

The tickets catch my eye and I pick up the paper. Am I doing the right thing by leaving? I have no idea what I'll be facing, or what demons will be waiting for me, but I can't stay in this non-life. I have to change from the path I'm on and getting away is the only way that will happen. It has to the right thing. I need to be the version of me that Aria deserves. I have to be present in her life because she is my whole fucking world. She needs to know how important she is to me, because nothing I've done so far shows her anything other than that I am a drunken waste of fucking space. Nothing. I've let her down over and over and she's never pulled me up on it. She just loves me. I don't deserve it.

I yawn. I'm so fucking tired. My body aches from all the chaos and the scars still pull on my stomach reminding me of the final descent into hell. I know that it wasn't just the whiskey bottle that has cut me to shreds, the vitriolic voices did too, shrieking at me from the depths of my broken mind. Their constant reminders of my failings trapped me in a void so bleak I thought I would die there. So many wasted opportunities to rise back up because of the fearsome hold that my father has over me, a hold so fucking tight that it allowed him to take everything from me. Am I always to be *fucking little shit, should never have been born* or is there a way out? By leaving, will I find the way? I fucking hope so. I'm putting all my faith into it being what I need so I can't consider that it won't be. I can't think about failing because there will be nothing if I do. There will be no way back to Molly. I wonder what she is doing now. I wonder if she's thinking about me and if she'll ever forgive me.

In this lonely existence, wondering is all I can do.

Molly

Oh my God, why did I say yes to the job offer? Why didn't I just accept the next commission for furniture refurb and the meeting with a prospective client who wanted to talk over the ideas she has for her apartment in the Royal Crescent? I should have just done that. Not be heading down to a hotel that needs complete renovation and, knowing my luck, rebuilding. What the fuck do I know about project managing on this scale? Nothing, that's what. Nothing. Holy shit, I must be mad.

Why didn't I decline, politely say, *thanks but no thanks* and just left another interior designer to do it. One who is qualified! Hell, I've not even finished my diploma! Ella thinks it's all marvellous and it will be the making of my business but right now it just feels as though another huge wave is coming for me! The three million quid I'm responsible for terrifies me, and it's sitting in my bank account where it's been ever since I met with Jonny's lawyer and accountant. They think he's mad. I could see it in the hesitancy to hand over the paperwork and now I've signed on the dotted line so it's all on me.

"Fuck." I mumble, stuffing the file with details of insurance, alarm codes, online banking and all sorts into my bag along with my laptop. What was Jonny thinking entrusting me with it all. Bloody idiot.

I walk out of the bedroom with the bag and my small suitcase. The flat seems so quiet. I've lived here alone for several weeks, and I still can't quite believe it's all mine. Paul collected his things and now there is no sign that he was ever here. Photos of us have been put back in albums and stored in the lounge cupboard where all the memorabilia of my life are kept. I've put up a photo of Corey and me, his young, handsome face smiling out of the frame. It's nice to be able to miss him. To visit his grave and to spend time with his mum and not have to brace myself for the snide comments from Paul. The picture of Jonny I kept from the magazine is taped to the fridge. I should have just thrown it away but I'm not ready to. I'm not ready to accept that I may never see him again.

I hear a car pull up to the kerb and a horn beeps in short, sharp toots. Ella is here. It's time to go. Hells bells. I cross the lounge to the corridor that leads to the bathroom and liberally add toilet cleaner to the bowl and close the blind. I feel a pang. I've no idea when I'll next see my flat. I'm on the road to the unknown, and I'm apprehensive. No, screw that, I'm terrified.

✳✳✳

"I can't leave you here!" Ella says, her face full of horror. "It's disgusting! it stinks! It's in the middle of nowhere!" She spins around on the tiled reception floor. "There's a desk holding the front door in place! Oh my God, Molly, you could end up murdered in your bed and no one would ever know."

"Don't be silly," I reply, far more lightly that I actually feel. In the cold light of day, the damage to the hotel is infinitely worse than I remember. "I'm perfectly safe!"

"Safe? Are you mad? There is nothing safe about this place! It needs condemning."

I agree with her, not that I plan on saying that out loud. The front door is hanging on by one hinge and some randomly nailed on bits of wood. The desk is pushed back up against it to keep the building secure, where it had been during the storm. It was fine being here alone when I had Jonny and the weather to keep anyone out, but I'm starting to feel panic. The peninsula is isolated, and the restaurant next door is still closed. I didn't go as far as the development kitchen, but the glass was still broken so I guess no one is there either.

"You cannot stay here on your own, Molly. It's awful. It could fall down around your ears and you'd be buried alive and it would be my fault for leaving you here!"

"It's not going to fall down."

"It stinks, you'll get some nasty, incurable disease..."

"Ella, you are overdramatising, calm down. I won't die, I won't get sick, I won't get buried. I will be fine." I say more for my benefit than hers. "Besides, I won't be on my own for long. The contractors will be here in a couple of weeks to empty it all and start repairing the building, and besides, the town is ten minutes away, I can always check in to a hotel there if it does start falling down around my ears."

Ella looks at me crossly. "It's not funny, Molly, this is so much worse than you'd let on."

"You're worrying unnecessarily. The quiet will do me some good. There is a pool, the utilities work and there is a full bar, so it will be fine!" I hope I sound more confident than I feel, although the look on Ella's face makes me unconvinced. "Come on, let me show you around."

"I'm not sure I want to. I may catch something."

"All you're likely to catch is a fish, stop worrying!"

"Why would there be a fish?"

"Because the water came up to here!" I show her the water marks on the steps that lead from the reception to the bar.

"I still can't believe you nearly died," she whispers and then to my horror Ella bursts into tears. "Fucking Paul and his shit present. I could have lost you forever because of him." I wrap my arms around her.

"But you didn't. I'm still here." I say softly.

"Only just." She shudders and squeezes me so tightly I swear a rib cracked.

Yeah, it was 'only just' but I can't look back on that terrifying time without believing that it was all meant to be. Finding the will to survive, finding Jonny and realising that my time with Paul had come to an end was all part of my journey through this crazy life. There are always lessons to be learned, new paths to walk down and this small area of the world showed me where I needed to be to find my peace. My heart is here, with the broken, unhappy man who gave me sanctuary inside the damp, grey walls but I left stronger than when I arrived, even if my heart broke in the process.

"I will be fine," I tell Ella, standing back and wiping her tears with the cuff of Jonny's hoodie. "This is where I need to be. I love this hotel. I love what it will become."

She looks at me and concedes. "Alright, I'll go along with this insanity, but you have to promise that you'll text me every hour of every day so I know you're not buried under a pile of rubble!"

"Every hour?"

"Every single one!"

I sigh, "ok, I'll do it!"

"Good girl."

***

"How can one person win all these?" Ella asks amazed, looking into the library cupboard where Jonny has stashed his awards. "Sexiest Man Alive! Really?"

"He actually is!" I say taking it from her. "There is something about him that...I dunno, it is something that can't be faked. It's like he glows. Even though he was so sad when I met him, and so lost, there is a glow that pulls you to him."

"You've got it bad!" Ella laughs, "I've never seen you like this."

"If you'd met him, you'd understand."

"You know, Moll, I think I'm one of the lucky ones," she says, setting the award down. "Since I met Robbie, I've just been happy. Sure, he annoys me and sometimes he's such a slob, but I'm just happy. It's not fireworks all the time, and the air around him doesn't vibrate with something magical, but I look at him and he's mine and it makes me feel content with my lot. I think I'm lucky."

"You are lucky," I nod my head in agreement. "But he's the really lucky one and he knows it. I love the way he looks at you, like he's won the lottery, and that you always come first with him. Even when he's drunk and his mates are around, it's only ever about you. He's one of life's good ones, Ella."

"It's what I want for you." She says softly. "For you to have a good one. You never glowed with Paul, that's how I knew he wasn't the one." Ella sighs, "but I worry that you will spend too much time waiting for Jonny, when all he has done is hide behind the gift of your flat and giving you this job."

"I'm not waiting!" I reply, not meeting her eye.

"You can deny it all you want but you know you are! Just protect yourself Molly, life is precious and it's short. I don't want to dissect every single thing he's ever said to you, because I still don't understand the workings of a male brain, but while I may have a feeling about Jonny, you still have to live. Don't get lost here."

"What feeling do you have?" I ask, looking at her.

Ella rolls her eyes. "Silence speaks volumes sometimes Moll, but even so, please don't put your life on hold."

"I won't. I've got too much to do anyway. This hotel won't decorate itself."

"You're not planning on painting the whole thing on your own?" She asks, her eyes widening.

I giggle, "oh God, no! The decorators are coming! All I plan to do is paint the hideous dark furniture and put pictures up. I'd never come out alive if I had to paint every wall!"

"Oh thank God, I was beginning to panic that you'd never come back to Bath!"

"Of course I'll come back!"

She stares at me, "your face says otherwise!"

"Ignore my face, it does that!" I laugh at her, "I have to be honest, all the way down here I was hoping you'd just turn round and take me home."

"I can just take you home." She says.

"I can't though, Ella. Now that I'm here I feel so excited to have been given this chance. It's a blank canvas that I can put my stamp on, I mean, how many new interiors businesses get something like this come along? I really want to make it feel to others how it feels to me…"

"Trashed?"

"Haha, no! Somewhere to feel safe. To rediscover something that got lost. Somewhere to fall in love and find peace and everything in between. It probably sounds crazy to want to make a place look like all of that, but that's what I see when I look at it."

"It sounds perfect," she says smiling softly at me, "and I have faith in you being able to do it because you are so amazingly talented. You light up when you talk about it but even so, I still don't want to leave you here, just in case it falls down."

"It won't fall down! I might..."

"That's a given!"

***

I spread the boards out on the bar while Ella pours us a glass of wine. "Are these your ideas?" She asks, handing me a glass and picking up one of the boards. "For in here?"

"Yes." I worked on the plans at home, from the memories I had from my time here. The boards are a mix of pictures cut out from magazines, fabric swatches, paint samples and wallpaper snips. I've worked on each of the rooms downstairs. They're not exact but I like the looks, they're calm and fresh. "What do you think?"

"I love them, this one in particular - " Ella lifts the board with my vision for the library. "I can see what you meant about the light in there and this looks fab."

"It was the room where I knew things had changed for me," I say, "I wanted it to look like that feeling of freedom. Do you think it does?"

"It definitely does." She grins at me, "I knew you were amazing but honestly, Molly, I'd no idea you were so talented. I mean, I've seen you repainting furniture, but these are something else. I can actually see the rooms in my head, you're so clever, my friend, so, so clever. I'm in awe of you seeing beyond this mouldy shithole and being inspired to do these! Where are you going to start?"

"Well, I'm going to do an itinerary of each room, make notes on what can be salvaged and given new life, and sort what needs to be thrown out. The skips are coming tomorrow and the company who is stripping everything out will start in a couple of weeks, so this is the calm before the chaos!"

"It's just as well you have a full bar!" She says, "you'll need it! What are you going to do for fun because you can't just work!"

"I will carry on looking for Jonny's missing money…"

"That doesn't sound like fun!"

"It's not really, but it will keep me occupied because there is only so much shit tv a girl can watch! I may even walk on the beach and face my fear head on…" From out of nowhere I burst into loud, noisy, snotty tears. "I can't seem to escape it, Ella. Every time I close my eyes I can see the wave coming for me but worse than that, I miss him," I sob, burying my face in my hands, "I miss him so much and when I wake up from a nightmare, the pain of missing him literally takes my breath away. I know it will get better and I will stop feeling like this, but my ego has been bruised and it hurts. He probably doesn't even think about me and here I am blubbing over him like some fucking idiot."

"I'm sure he thinks of you," Ella says, handing me some blue catering tissue. "He'd be fool not to, you're so awesome and I reckon he thinks that too. Everything he's done says it with a big red bow."

"I'm just going to have to trust the universe," I sniff, wiping my face with the tissue, "and work hard. Prove to myself that I can do this, even if it feels really overwhelming." A shudder takes my voice and I whisper, "sorry, I'm a dick!"

"Yeah, you are, but you're my most favourite dick, well, after Robbie's of course!"

I laugh and screw the tissue up. "Fill up my glass, Ella, that comment has left a nasty taste in my mouth."

"Sometimes it leaves a nasty taste in mine too."

I throw the tissue at her and she laughs before falling silent. "You've got this, my precious friend, you've got everything you need and while I don't want you to sit and pine for him, I think he may just be pining for you too."

"I hope so, Ella, I really, really hope so."

Jonny

The train porter shows me to my seat and stores my small suitcase on the rack. I sink down into the soft leather and put my feet up on the seat opposite. I feel tired. Bone fucking tired. And uneasy. I'm so uncertain of this being the right thing to do. It feels like I'm running away rather than running forwards but I'm holding onto the hope that I will find what I'm looking for. Fucking peace mainly. Some time away from the noise, and away from the battle with Chelsea that I fear is coming. She wants to take me for everything I have and more. I'm sad that I took her down with me. Chelsea isn't a bad person, she just had a tough start in life and wants to be more than that. She had it for a while, but now she's on her own. I hope she thrives. I hope she finds what she's looking for and that her next lover is decent. I'm not sure he will be, but I can hope.

Being sober has made me look back at my marriage with a different view. I took the blame, took the vitriol and revulsion and let her yell all sorts at me because I was so disgusted with what I'd become. I take a long breath in and wince as the scars on my stomach pull. They have healed but are still a reminder of what I was. Drunk. Wasted. Waster. Broke. Broken. I was all of those things until Molly came along. What I want to do is run back to her, ask her to forgive me for being a huge fucking dick, take her to bed and build my future with her. Only, I can't because she deserves so much more than what I have to give her right now. I need to work on myself to be worthy of her, but if I could get off this train and go to her, I would.

"Can I get you a drink?" The waitress asks standing by my chair. Whiskey, I think, a large whisky.

"Cola please, with lots of ice."

"Sure. Anything to eat?" She hands me a laminated menu and I choose some items. She gives me a lingering smile and then says, "I'm not supposed to ask but can I have a selfie?"

"Of course." She crouches down beside me and takes her phone from the pocket of the apron she's wearing. I smile. She pouts.

"Thanks." She says looking at the picture. "I recognised you from the tv."

"Oh, that's nice." I reply, noncommittedly. I don't know what else to say.

"I'll get your order now."

I smile my thanks. Another couple of passengers board the train and take their seats. I pull the cap down on my head and shift my position so I'm looking out of the window, with my back half to them. The waitress brings my drink and food, before moving to the others. I watch as people mingle on the platform, some running for their train, others boarding this one and one couple, who share a long, deep kiss. Loneliness twists my heart until it seems to stop beating. This has to work. Leaving has to the right decision because it's too painful to consider that this is going to be the biggest fucking mistake of my life.

✳✳✳

The train rolls into Glasgow mid-afternoon and I wearily heave myself up out of seat. Five hours of staring mindlessly out of the window, buoyed only by endless coffee and colas, has left me feeling low and shaky. The voices that usually taunt me have been surprisingly quiet, but their absence makes me nervous. What is coming? What monumental fucking torment is going to hit me?

"Mr Raven?" The porter comes along the aisle. "Your train to Fort William is due at seventeen hundred from Glasgow Queen Street station, which is a ten minute walk."

He hands me a local map. "There is plenty to do in the city for the next few hours, if you'd like some recommendations?"

"No thanks, I'll be fine."

"Then good afternoon to you."

"Thank you, and to you."

The train waitress loiters in the corridor by the door. She bites her lip, freshly painted in red lip colour, and smiles coyly at me. "I've got a few hours off, fancy some company?"

Once upon a time the train wouldn't have left the station before I'd have seduced her and fucked her in the toilet, but her obvious attempt at being sexy is a turnoff. What the fuck is wrong with me? It's been months since I had a shag, and the last time was a miserable experience. I was pissed on whiskey and Chelsea was watching tv over my shoulder so neither of us finished anyway. Perhaps a quick fuck would boost the ego, but what if I'm shit, and I've forgotten what to do. I hold back a smirk. Of course, I know what to do, I did it enough – hundreds of women, thousands probably, their faces blurring into one.

"Thanks, but not today."

"Are you sure," she runs her polished nail up my arm. It doesn't make her any more fuckable.

"Yes," I pick up my case from the rack, "I'm sure."

She mutters something under her breath as I leave the train. The truth is that the only person I want to sleep with is Molly and I screwed that up. I hope she knows why.

I kill time walking around Glasgow. I did a few shows here back in the day, but I didn't see much of the city. I stop for a coffee then shop for some cheap joggers and hoodies. I don't get recognised by anyone, thank God. Social media doesn't need any more of my failings, the magazine was bad enough. I pick up a couple of books that catch my eye in a shop then head to the train station, handing over my ticket to board the train. Nerves prickle in my stomach. What the fuck

82

am I going to find? I have a castle, a fucking castle, that I've never seen. A castle that has been looked after by a couple who have never once contacted me for money, or anything related to its upkeep. I wish Molly was here with me holding my hand which would be really fucking welcome right about now. The train pulls away from the station and I'm overcome by anxiety. I have no idea who the caretakers are, or what they know about me. Our correspondence has been one email to say I was coming and one reply to say they'd meet me. That's it. I could be walking into a horror movie with crazy people who have been locked in a Scottish castle for twenty-five years.

For the entire hour on the train, I want to turn back. Go back to Cornwall and take Molly in my arms but when the train slows into the small station, I stand up, collect my bags and get off. My heart thuds painfully in my chest. What the fuck am I doing? Each foot step along the platform feels heavier and heavier until I reach the exit. Fear rolls down my face in sweaty droplets and damp patches form under my arms. I can't breathe. I can't fucking breathe. Holy fuck, I'm going to have a panic attack. Holy, holy fuck, Molly where are you? Molly? Molly? Slippery hands tear at the neckline of the tee-shirt I'm wearing. Oh my God. My throat. My throat is closing. Why can no one see? Why have I come here? I should be in Cornwall. I can't heal myself, I'm a disgusting, broken drunk, I'm *that fucking kid who should never have been born.*

"Mr Raven?" A kind looking woman with short silver hair and grey rimmed glasses steps forward and smiles at me. "Mr Raven, I'm Julie Brown." She speaks with a soft Scottish accent and her bright blue eyes sparkle. "I thought I'd come and meet you here, rather than you taking a taxi to the castle. Are you alright? You look a little grey."

"I'm not feeling so good."

"A long day, I expect." She says, taking my case. I don't try and stop her. "It's a fair old way from London to here and there are another couple of hours to get to the castle. I reserved you a room in a guest house just up the road, in case you didn't want to travel any further today. Your train is later than I expected so perhaps you would prefer to set out tomorrow?"

"That's a good idea," I mumble, ridiculously grateful for her kindness.

"They do evening meals so no need to worry about where to eat."

"What about you?" I ask. I sound strangled, my tongue feeling thick in my mouth.

"I've booked myself and Mark, that's my husband, rooms too." Julie guides me towards a small battered green car. "Probably not the luxurious car you're used to," she grins, "but it does us."

"I don't have a car, so you're one up on me!" I tell her. "Until fairly recently, I didn't even know I had a castle." My head is banging as though I've woken with the worst hangover.

"I'm still trying to work out how you forgot you owned it!"

"I spent too much time drunk and had more money than sense!"

Julie laughs. "So, it was a big surprise then!"

"Surprise is an understatement." My heart suddenly sinks. "Do I owe you any pay? I have no idea about that."

"No, our pay came out of the maintenance account. I've paid for the hotel from it too, I assumed it would be ok?"

"There's an account?"

"Yes, you set it up when you employed us to look after the property."

"I did?"

"Just how much did you drink, Mr Raven?" Julie asks incredulously.

"You really don't want to know."

Molly

My laptop beeps and wakes me from a strange dream where I was walking down the aisle in an aqua-green bikini to marry Paul before a huge, grey wave ripped through the church and dragged me away. I feel disorientated by the darkness for a moment or two, until I realise that I'm in Cornwall and the streetlight I'm so used to seeing peeping through my curtains is back in Bath.

I rub sleep from my eyes and wriggle up to sitting, yawning. I'd forgotten how comfortable the bed was in my suite, but instead of rolling back into the comfort I fling the covers back and get up, stretching my whole body as I do. I slept too well, and my limbs feel sluggish and uncoordinated as I stumble across the room to the coffee table where my computer sits. I've been running a programme to look for Jonny's money and the beep can only mean one thing. Something has been found.

I pull his hoodie over my pyjamas and put on the one pair of fluffy socks that I packed and pick up the laptop. I leave the suite and wander downstairs, flicking on lights as I go, the soft light at odds with the lingering smell of damp and fishy sea water. I open the window in reception to let in some air and look out at the night with its navy-blue sky and twinkling stars that sit like tiny spotlights. I wonder if Jonny is somehow looking up at the same sky and thinking of me, or if he's fallen into a barrel of whiskey. I hope not. I hope he finds a way breaks the hold his father has on him and rise back up to the glory he once had. I stare up at the inky night trying to let the sadness go, but it keeps hold and eventually the cold draws me back and I walk along the corridor to the kitchen to make a pot of coffee before taking everything to Jonny's office.

It's still a mess but somehow it makes me feel better that it is. I spent a lot of time in this room, and it feels like a safe place in amongst the huge task ahead of me. I flop down into the chair and put my feet up on the desk, my eyes falling onto the pile of files still haphazard on the floor from where I tripped over. I don't want the image of me gazing up at Jonny, looking into his silver wolf eyes as he catches me, replaying over and over but it's like a broken film tape and I can't turn it off. That was the moment I thought he would kiss me. The breath catching in both our throats, neither moving... but it wasn't. That came later and then I was left out in the cold.

Fuck it.

I push some of the mess on the desk to one side and open the computer programme and watching the functions light up. "Ok, Platform, what have you found?"

I type my password onto the Platform programme, and it runs numbers down the screen before before formatting into a document with a single account number. "Holy fuck." I sit bolt upright, knocking the coffee mug over. There it is. The link to the missing money. It's not a number I recognise from the UK or EU, so I open another programme, type the number in and wait. I must have nodded off because the beep from my laptop jolts me upright. I wipe my mouth clean of drool and roll my shoulders, clicking the access information. The account has been found in – I type it into peer at the screen. "Where the fuck is that?"

The number flashes at me over and over. I pull the laptop closer and google the country. It's on the other side of the world. How do you open a bank account on the other side of the world and forget about it?

"He forgot he owned a castle and half a gaming business," I mutter, "what else has he forgotten?" I flick my fingernails with my thumbs and think. How am I going to get into an account in a country I've never heard of. I press a few keys on the laptop and set another banking programme running. I feel inquisitive now, wondering what else I can find. It wouldn't hurt to look, to see if there is anything else I can uncover, while I wait for the banking programme to open, if it will. The programmes purr and the laptop screen goes dark, so I use the time to make another coffee and open a packet of biscuits I find in the larder. Through the kitchen window the day is beginning to wake up with dawn peeping from under the darkness. I do a couple of yoga poses to ease the stiffness in my back, I must have dozed for longer than I'd realised.

While the coffee brews I think about the options. There is an account which means there is money because a person doesn't open an account in a country where no one will think to look, if it's not to hide big sums of cash. And if there is a big sum of cash, who do I tell? His shit accountant? The lawyer who looked down his nose at me? I don't know how to get hold of Jonny so perhaps it will be ok to wait, I mean, he's been without it for twenty years, another few months won't matter, will it? I could demand his number from the lawyer or the accountant but then, what would I say if he answered. *Hi Jonny, I know things are weird but thanks for my house and the job but also, I may have just found your money.* Fuckity fuck fuck.

I could leave it all on his desk when I finish working here, and he'd never have to even speak to me. Three days with Jonny and a lifetime without. My heart actually hurts, like a weight has taken up residence on my chest and is getting heavier by the minute. "This is not rational, Molly, you're being insane," I mutter, before storming out of the kitchen and heading towards the pool. I turn the lights on and strip off my clothes, jumping naked into the dark blue water, no longer scared of what lurks beneath the surface. *I'll jump with you. I've got you.* Ella's right. He's done all he is able to do. He's given me my home and given me this project which I am grateful for, but I would swap it all for one more day. Just one. With him. Here, with the storm raging

88

outside, safely locked away from the world. Just him and me. I would give it all up for that.

***

"Have you been awake all night?" Ella asks, sleepily wandering into the kitchen.

"Not all night."

"You look tired."

"I am, I'm waiting for the caffeine to kick in, but so far this is my fourth cup," I gesture to the mug in my hand, "and nothing has happened yet."

"You'll have the shakes soon enough," she comments picking up a mug and pouring a coffee from the cafetiere. "Why didn't you sleep?"

"I was having a weird dream about Paul, then my laptop pinged, and it woke me up. Thank God. I was going to marry him in a bikini..."

"Paul was in a bikini, hells bells, what an image!" Ella blows on her coffee then takes a sip.

"I was the one in the bikini." I grin, "post-trauma crazy dream! Anyway, I got up when the laptop started beeping and did some work on Jonny's missing money, and guess what, I found an account, overseas, in a country I had to google!"

"Did you? How much did you find?"

"I don't know yet, I've had to set another programme running to try and access the account. I'm not sure how successful I'll be, because it's outside of every banking agreement I know of. I feel like I need to have all the answers before I tell anyone what I've found."

Ella looks thoughtful, "is that so you can be thorough or so that he'll whisk you up into his arms and snog your face off?"

I laugh, "perhaps a little of both!"

"Imagine forgetting where you put your money," she says slurping her coffee. "If I had enough money that I could lose it, I'd be wearing it, not hiding it in the Caribbean!"

I laugh, "There are only so many shoes…"

"Wash your mouth out," Ella says with faux outrage, "there are never enough shoes."

Ella's obsessive relationship with shoes began when she found a pair of 1920s shoes in a charity shop in Bath. They were low heeled, patent leather and smelt like they'd been buried in cow pat, but she loved them and wore them until they completely fell apart. We were twelve at the time and had just been allowed to go into Bath on our own, on the bus, from our houses in Combe Down. They'd cost her all the pocket money she'd saved for months and months. From there, the shoe obsession grew and grew and now she has more than she can count. She loves them all. Sometimes I wish I was as cool and funky as Ella, but fashion has passed me by. I'm thirty and I'm beige.

"I'm so beige." I grumble, breaking a biscuit in half and dipping it into my coffee. Ella is right, with all the sugar and caffeine I've had this morning, I'll be shaking for weeks.

"You're not beige!" She grins, "you're fiery and full of light, you're golden, Moll. Definitely not beige. Although," she looks me up and down, "you really need to find something other than that hoodie to wear, you've not worn anything else for weeks."

"I know, but…" I feel my face flood with embarrassment.

"But your one true love gave it to you and now you can't possibly take it off," Ella interrupted, laughing. "It's the thing you do, wear their clothes! Do you remember when Corey bought that horrible bright green hoodie with white embossed writing on it, I can't remember the brand, but it cost him loads and it was awful. You wore it for weeks and weeks until his Mum asked for it back! You're such a *teenager* Moll!"

90

"I am, aren't I! Thirty going on fifteen and I know I should put it back in his room, but I don't want to take it off! Although, if you were standing in a boy's hoodie being all wet like me, I'd be looking at you like you're looking at me and suggest you take it off too!" I sip my coffee. "I know what I look like, Els, it's all a bit embarrassing really, but hey ho, I can't help it. He's got under my skin."

"Yeah well," she says, topping up her mug, "you're under his too, so what will be will be. I have faith."

"I'm glad you do." I mutter. "I don't have faith in anything other than damp bricks and mess. Everything squelches! I'm wondering how the contractors will get on with taking it all out, it's going to be revolting!"

"Surely they know what to expect. They're not walking into this shit hole thinking it's going to a cute little boutique hotel for rich folk?"

"Oh no, they are absolutely aware of how grim it all is. They've been out and met with the hotel general manager, because apparently, I'm not qualified to listen!" I raise an eyebrow and Ella laughs.

"I bet they didn't have the balls to say that to your face?"

"Of course not! The firm is a local one, something to do the with the general manager - brother or brother-in-law or something - and their reputation is really good. I had a chat with them on the phone and their price was excellent, plus they didn't need to live in, and all the other contractors did, so it suited me. However, despite my fabulous interview and negotiating skills I wasn't involved in the meeting because Jonny's accountant arranged for them to come out when I wasn't here, so the GM sorted it all. He hates me!"

"Who? The GM?"

"No, the accountant! I know he has a job to do, to keep Jonny's money safe from the assumed frivolous spending I'm going to be doing but honestly, he is the most condescending arse I've ever met. He told me I had to send all the expenditure receipts weekly by special delivery. Like I will be able to traipse in and out of town without a car. It makes me feel so untrusted. Plus, he's shit at his job, because if he was any good, he'd have sorted Jonny's missing money by now."

Ella steers me away from my rant. "So, what did the contractors decide?"

"There aren't any structural problems, it's mainly just fixing holes in windows, patching up ceilings, replastering and rebuilding the conservatory. The big job is clearing out all the carpets and stripping wallpaper, but that's their task, mine is to make everything look nice!"

"It can't look worse, to be fair!" Ella laughs, "it's so dreary."

"It is now, but it won't be, it'll be the place everyone wants to come."

"I love your faith!"

I grin, "the look on your face says something else!"

"I just don't want to leave you here alone! The doors barely stand up, what is someone breaks in! Can't you stay in town and just drive in every day?"

"My car is in at the scrap yard!"

"Oh yes, I forgot about that! Are you really sure you're happy to be here alone?" Ella asks, looking up at the hole in the kitchen ceiling. "It's so grim!"

"Yes," I say, fiddling with the little radio until I find a station. I still find it strange that a kitchen like this still uses a portable radio rather than have a smart system. Not that I'm complaining, the little radio was a godsend in the storm. "I'll be fine. What's the worst that can happen?"

"I can think of plenty?"

"Nah! You're worrying too much," I say lightly.

Ella shakes her head, "the more of this place I see, the more I think you're nuts."

"It will be filled with contractors before I know it." I find a station and the little radio fills the room with tinny sounding pop. "I love this song."

"Your music taste is the worst!"

I laugh, "you're not the first person to tell me that!" The memory sucks the light away for a moment. His energy is here, I can feel him, hear his voice in the breeze that whistles in the gaps left by the storm. I wonder if I'll ever see him again, if we will cross paths and what it will be like when we do. Would it be awkward, hesitant, would I feel embarrassed by the rejection, or would he smile, and I'll forget it all.

"Earth to Molly!" Ella's voice jolts me from my thoughts, and I contort my face into a smile. "Can you stop mooning over your lost love for a moment, I'm starving!"

***

Ella has gone and I'm all alone in the crumbling building. Despite my bravado about the solitude, the reality is suddenly so much different. I walk around the hotel checking that all the outside doors are secure against any unwanted visitors then return to Jonny's office. The fan on my laptop is whirring loudly and when I lay my hand on it, it's boiling.

"Shit." I push the window open and put the laptop up on the sill. The sun hasn't moved around to the side of the building so the spot is cool, I pray that my laptop survives the effort of searching. I leave the office and open the door to the GM's room. It's much tidier than Jonny's with rows of files on shelves against the wall. I sit down at the desk and pull out my phone, dialling a number.

"Hi Damon, it's Molly, remember me from Forage Forensics?" I ask when the call is answered.

"Hi Molly," Damon says cheerfully, "of course I do."

"Marvellous! How are you?"

"Good thank, Molly. What can I do for you?"

"I'm running a series of programmes on my laptop but it's sounding a little like a rocket about to take off. I was wondering if I could add the programmes to a desktop."

"Let me check your laptop, is it with you now?"

I run back to Jonny's office and collect my laptop, following Damon's instructions to allow him access.

"Leave it with me, I'll ring you when I've checked it over. I may be able to do some magic."

We say our goodbyes and I take my coffee to reception to look out at the flat, blue ocean. The scene before me is unrecognisable to the savagery of my last visit. The calm day is inviting and the warmth of the high sun rests on my face. I rest my coffee mug on the window sill and wrestle with the desk still holding the front door secure. Someone is coming to fix it today, thank God. It takes me some time to hook the door against the wall and I have to give it a kick to finally get it all the way back. The fresh air comes rushing in and it's a relief from the mouldy smell, which seems to be worsening. I can't wait for all the soggy carpets to be removed in hope they take the bad smell with them.

I walk down the steps to the driveway. I've not explored the grounds and I'm intrigued to see what land surrounds the hotel, and what state it is in. I look down at the sea road scanning for the supermarket van, until I'm momentarily stopped in my tracks by the unwelcome memory of the moments before The Kiss. "Go away Jonny." I groan, closing my eyes but it's his face I see, looking down at me. I can feel his cool breath on my cheek and the scent of his body wrapping itself around me. I expect him to be stood in front of me because I can still feel him. I can still smell the citrus essence of him and a pull so strong that I could be back battling the current for survival.

"Oh, fuck off." I hiss and stomp along the driveway as though angry footsteps will make everything better.

94

The evidence of the storm is all around. Branches, torn from the trees, litter the ground, and where grass used to be there are now vast brown patches spreading out across the front garden. Divots still sit on the bank where the water climbed the hill and washed away again. It all looks like a disaster zone, and I make a mental note to review the landscaping quotes to get someone started as soon as possible.

I follow the driveway around to the car park and take an uneven, bricked path, beyond the trashed flower beds. The path winds through bushes that have been dragged from the ground, past a pond filled with leaves and flower heads, and onto the garden at the rear of the hotel. The sun beams down which makes the devastation look worse. I continue past the library window, past the restaurant and eventually I reach the old chapel that houses the spa and pool. Despite its current state the garden has so much potential. Bubbles of excitement run up my spine. This place is going to be spectacular.

I walk around the outside of the chapel, taking care not to stand on any of the gravestones that pepper the ground on the west side of the building. I'm hesitant. A number of headstones have fallen, and the soil looks thin that I'm half expecting the dead to rise up. I shiver and run along the path to the front of the hotel. Someone else can check that the residents of the afterlife are where they should be, not me, I've seen too many scary movies to go checking on the wellbeing of the dead.

I stand on the drive looking up at the imposing grey building. I have to get this right. There is something so special about this place, whether that's because it saved me from certain death, or because I fell in love here - whatever it is, it's all wrapped up in the soft grey embrace.

"You've got this, Molly." I tell myself, running my hand through my short hair and when a roof tile falls to the ground, a laugh explodes out of me. "Maybe you don't 'got this'!"

I turn to walk back into the building but the supermarket delivery coming up the drive slows me.

"Hello," I say as the driver exits his cab.

"Afternoon." He replies.

"Lovely day."

"Yes," he says with a finality that doesn't require any more conversation from me. He stacks the bags up at the front door and drives off without a goodbye.

"Charming," I grumble, taking the bags up the steps, stopping to wrestle the front door closed before walking through the hotel to the kitchen. Once the bags are unloaded into the kitchen, I pour a glass of wine. It feels like wine o'clock, and with no one here to pull a face, I make it a large one and take it to the library. I turn on the speakers and let the playlist flood the space. This is still my favourite room, despite the damp, peeling wallpaper and smell of wet carpet. There is a light in here that feels different to the rest of the hotel. The cupboard door swings open in a draught and the gold glints from inside. I put my wine down on the small side table and take the awards from the cupboard. The Sexiest Male ones make me smile. How true they are. Jonny is the sexiest man I've ever seen. I sigh and pull out the ones further back. So many gold statues, framed discs and plaques all saying the same thing - Jonny was a unique talent. He can be again, I'm sure of it but as for now, I just hope he's alright, wherever he is.

I spill wine down the front of the hoodie when my phone rings from inside the pocket. "Hi Damon," I answer, brushing away the spill with my hand, "is it sorted?"

"Yep, it sure is!" He replies cheerfully, and then reels off all the techy things he's done to my laptop.

"You're amazing, thank you." I say, walking across the library, "I'm just going to check it now."

"I'll hang on the phone while you do," he says, "but, you know Molly, you really need to move your files onto the cloud, it's the reason things are running so slowly."

"I'm not so good at admin," I admit grinning.

"I noticed!" I can hear his smile down the phone.

"Cheeky!" I reply, lifting the laptop onto the desk. He tells me what to do and I follow the instructions, before clicking the final 'enter' for the programme to conclude. My mouth falls open as I stare at the screen. Holy fuck.

"All ok?" Damon asks. I've no idea how long I've been silent for.

"All good, thank you, Damon, you've been a star but, without being rude, I have to go."

"It's a big sum!"

"It is…Shit. Ummm, thanks so much for helping me, I owe you, but…sorry Damon, I need to go, I…uh…bye Damon," I stammer, my eyes fixed to the number in the box. What do I do now? Who do I call? I stare for moments longer before selecting another number in my phone.

"Ella," I say before she even has a chance to speak, "Ella, I've found it."

"Found what?"

"Jonny's missing money."

"No way! How much?"

"Eleven million, two hundred and sixty thousand, fifty-seven pounds…" I put my hands on my heart to try and slow the frantic thumping. "What the fuck do I do now?"

"Ring Jonny!" She says excitedly, "ring him and be all fabulous. You've literally saved him from being destitute! He owes you big time."

"I don't have his number."

"Oh fuck."

"Yep, that just about sums it up."

"What are you going to do then," she asks. "Is there someone else you can call?"

"Only Jonny's accountant, but I really don't want to ring him, he's awful and besides, he should have found this years ago."

"Do nothing for now," Ella says thoughtfully, "there will be the right time, when all the stars align and you'll tell him, and he'll take you in his arms, snog your face off then shag your brains out..."

"I wish!" I laugh, "can you imagine how hot that would be?"

"Yuck," she mocks disgust, "I don't want to imagine anything of the sort, you filthy beast!"

I laugh, "seriously though, Ella, what should I do? I feel really shaky every time I look at the screen."

"I really think you should wait. You don't know how this story is going to unfold, and unless you can tell him person to person, then don't do anything. His accountant sounds like a total arse, and he shouldn't get any of the credit. Jonny has been without it for so long, a few more days, months, however long, won't make any difference. Have a drink..."

"I've got one."

"Have two!" Ella laughs, "or three, who will judge? All joking aside, though Moll, have you considered that you and Jonny were meant to meet to change each other's lives? Shit like this doesn't happen to just anyone."

"What, like fate, you mean?"

"Fate, the universe, the all-powerful creator, who knows! It just feels as though things are happening to you to make up a whole picture."

"Maybe." I say, "it would be nice to think so."

I can hear someone speak to her. "I have to go, Moll, I'm needed. I'll ring you tomorrow, ok? Be safe, drink lots, and stop staring at your laptop! Go and eat a gateau or something!"

"Bye Ella."

"Bye you luscious lush." Ella cancels the call and I sit for a while in the silence. The figure on the screen blinks at me.

"Well Jonny," I say to the room, "this is your lucky day, and you don't even know it."

I finish the wine in the glass and wander along the corridor to pour another, taking it outside. The sun is setting over the ocean and the soft breeze flutters the leaves that remain on the trees. I wish I knew what it all meant, all the upheaval and uncertainty that faces me, but maybe I'm not meant to know. Maybe the universe has other ideas, and my story is still being written. There's a safety in that idea and I feel a smile creep onto my face. Perhaps the best really is yet to come.

Jonny

My first thought is that Molly would love it.

The small square, yellow-bricked castle sits on an island that has been connected to the mainland by a yellow-bricked bridge. With the sun high behind it and a flat ocean it's picture-perfect and the isolation if the island is surprisingly just what my broken, lonely self needs. I grin when I consider the outrage from my former rock star self *what the fuck do you want to be in the middle of fucking nowhere for, you dick!*

"Is this your first time seeing it?" Julie asks, following my gaze.

"Yep." I slowly shake my head, "of all the strange things I've bought over the years, this has to be the strangest!"

She laughs. "You won't have to worry about stalkers all the way out there!"

"It's been a long time since I've had any, so no worries about crazy people!"

Julie looks at me with kindness in her eyes and I turn my head to avoid her gaze. I think she'll make me fucking bawl if she keeps being so nice. I'm glad when she changes the subject back to the castle.

"When the tide goes out you can walk directly across the sand to those steps over there, rather than taking the bridge which is the longer route. Although you need to watch tide times, it comes in quickly and it's a cold swim back!" She laughs. "The nearest village, well it's more of a town now, is a couple of miles in that direction -" she points up the coast path, "- it's a lovely walk, very blustery when the wind picks up but if you're looking to blow the cobwebs away then it'll suit you fine. The Thistle pub does wonderful food, proper hearty Scottish scran, all local, and The Wallace is more of a beer and scratchings sort of place. Both are great, it just depends what you want on the day."

"I think I just need to avoid people."

100

"Then you have the perfect place for that, but they're good people in town. They don't go in for fuss and celebrity so you wouldn't be bothered, but they'll quietly look out for you, if you let them."

"Are you from this area?"

"No, I'm from Glasgow. We moved here when we took the caretaker job." She shakes her head lightly, "I still can't believe you didn't remember you owned all this."

I laugh, "there is a lot I don't remember."

"We thought it was strange that we never heard from you. We did send annual accounts, and regular letters to the only address we had for you but there was never a reply. It was somewhere in London."

"I sold the London homes and if I ever had post with my old name on, which didn't happen a lot, it always went in the bin. I stopped being him a long, long time ago."

"That may explain why we couldn't find you when we looked you up." She shrugs, "We were looking under your old name because that's who you were when you gave us the job."

"I must have been absolutely wasted when I bought it because I stopped being John Jones just before I got really famous. I sometimes forgot that I'd changed my name when I'd been drinking! Did I meet you?"

"No. It was an interview on the phone, and it sounded loud where you were. The contract came handwritten with a red wine stain on it!"

"Sounds about right."

She rubs my arm in a motherly way, and I feel a wave of something painful begin to rise up. I swallow hard.

"That was the last we heard from you. Some bank forms came that we signed then we got a debit card, cheque book and access to a bank account with the castle's name on. I remember going to get a balance from the bank in Glasgow and there was more money than we'd ever seen just sitting in the account. We ran back to the car faster than the speed of light in case someone mugged us, and we drove up here." Julie laughs, "we needed a stiff drink, I can tell you!"

"What was it like here?"

"The castle wasn't in the best shape, but we did it up room by room. There was a lot of red tape with the listed buildings people, but we worked around that. It took a long time to make it habitable, but we think we've done a good job. There was no one to check if we were doing what you wanted us to do, so we just hoped for the best! Then you rang and we suddenly panicked that we'd got it all wrong!"

"I don't think I'm in any position to complain if it isn't!" I smiled, "if it wasn't for you and Mark, it would have probably crumbled into the sea!"

"For years, my husband was convinced you were the same person as the one who hired us and that we should contact your representation to check, but I didn't believe him." She grins, "I suppose he had to be right at least once in the last forty years, although he'll be reminding me of this until I'm in in the grave!"

I laugh, "it's probably just as well I've kicked the drink, no more random purchases!"

"When you see the home-brewed whiskey in the pub, you may not find sobriety so easy!"

"Oh hell, don't tell me that."

Julie laughs and pats my arm again, "the Highlands will look after you, you'll find something here you'll find nowhere else."

"Do you live in the castle?" I ask, tucking my hands in my pockets against the chill coming off the sea.

"No, we have a cottage five minutes' drive from here. The castle is beautiful, and we stayed for a little while but when I saw the cottage with the roses around the door, I just had to live there. Funny isn't it, what captures your heart?"

102

I think about Molly. Sweet, kind, pretty Molly. "Yes," I agree, "it is."

"Come on, Jonny, let me show you around the castle," Julie says opening the car door. I get into the front. Mark puts the car into gear and drives up to the stone bridge which is much grander than it looked from a distance. I can hear Molly's voice in my head, excited, full of enthusiasm and ideas, and the pang I have that she's not here with me is like a punch to the stomach. I may keep telling myself I did the right thing but the look on her face haunts my dreams and I miss her. I miss her face, her quiet ways, her wisdom. I just miss her.

"What do you think?" Julie asks as we drive through wrought iron gates at the end of the bridge and up to the huge wooden front door. Mark turns the engine off and the three of us get out of the car.

"I can't believe I own a castle, never mind one so grand. I suppose I expected it to be gloomy and cold but this-" I look up at the carved stone and the arched windows with the crisscrossed lead that holds the diamond-shaped panes "-is incredible. I have a friend who would take one look at this place and..." I fall silent. I don't want to imagine Molly's reaction. It's too painful because I know her well enough to know what she would say. What if coming here without her has been a mistake that I'll never be able to make up for?

"Jonny?" Julie prompts. "Do you want to go inside?"

I nod. Mark takes out a bunch of keys and unlocks the door, pushing it open. I step into the cool room.

"Fuck!" I say, looking around at the hall which stretches all the way up to the roof. Varnished balconies look over the hall and huge framed portraits sit on the walls up as far as the beams. "How did you get those up there?" I ask incredulously.

"Carefully." Mark says gruffly.

I walk across the flagstone floors, the soles of my shoes barely making a sound, opening the heavy doors that lead off the hall into endless other rooms - a long dining room, a small study, a library and so on, all immaculately clean and perfectly looked after. It's been loved. Completely different to what I left behind.

"I can't believe this." I say standing in the middle of the cosy snug that looks out over the sea. The ocean goes on forever, far beyond the mauve horizon line sitting on the top of the sparkling water. Fuck me. I could sit in this room all day and never be bored of the view. For the first time in weeks, I have real hope that I can mend. "I can't believe I've had this place for all these years. and it's completely passed me by. It would have made so much difference..." I fade off then surprisingly I laugh. It's a deep belly laugh that almost hurts as tears stream down my face.

How could I ever explain to anyone that finding out about these things makes me less broken, broke, fucked up, irrelevant and all the other words that have been used to describe me over the years. Julie looks at me like I've gone crazy, and I want to tell her that it's all just further proof that I was somebody, and that I could possibly be somebody again but I can't speak, I'm laughing too hard. Then, just as quickly as the laugh arrived, it's gone. I have no one to share this with. Like the battered building I left behind, it's not proof of greatness, however much I wish it was, it's just proof that I am alone. I am broken, lost, irrelevant and I have no one to share it with because I pushed the only woman that I've ever loved, away.

"You look sad," Julie comments as my laughter fades. "Are you not as happy with it as you first thought?"

"It's nothing like that. You have surpassed my expectations," I say, "I was just thinking..." I fall silent and sigh. "It doesn't matter what I was thinking, it had nothing to do with your incredible care of this building."

She puffs up her chest and beams, "come and see the rest of it, hopefully you will be just as pleased."

She guides me towards the staircase that sweeps up to the first floor. The balcony is bathed in the soft light that comes in from the huge window above the front door.

"The light is wonderful."

Molly's voice floats in my ear, *this place could be the sanctuary, a refuge and a retreat.*

Julie nods, "it is the same in every room which is the joy of being out here on the island. There is nothing to block the colours of the sky. Being a square building, the light seems different from each aspect but somehow it makes it more special. I love that you can see the sea from every window, but I like that there is a beach to walk on when the tide goes out. You just wait until the storms blow in, they are like nothing you will have ever seen before especially when the lightening forks down over the ocean, but there is something very magical about watching it."

"I've just been in a hellish storm. I'm hoping for sunshine now!"

"Ah, Jonny, I hate to tell you, but this is Scotland, storms are part of the charm!"

I laugh. "It's the same with Cornwall. Sunshine one minute, armageddon the next!" Except here no waif is going to wash up. I want to call her, tell her all about the castle, ask her to come and be with me, but I know I can't. I need to be the man she deserves if I'm ever going to fight for her.

I wander in and out of bedrooms with Julie giving me the history of the portraits and antiques that fill the rooms. Finally, she opens a small wooden door, and we climb the remaining flight of stairs coming to a stop in the attic. It's a huge square space that fills the roof of the castle, with windows under the eaves that give an almost complete 360 view of landscape. The ocean glints in its vastness to the west and the mountains stand tall in the east.

105

"Fuck me, look at this." I say, "you could fit a village in here!"

The attic has been divided into areas despite being open plan. There are music posters in frames on the walls and prints of my album covers on both sides of the chimney breast in the centre of the room. Overlooking the ocean is a music stand with an upright desk, more like an artist's easel and a pot of pens on a small shelf. Running under the window are five electric sockets. Beside the window that faces the mountains are two large arm chairs, a coffee table and a book shelf with note books lying flat, another pot of pens on the top. A large desk with two chairs is in front of the window facing south and in the north aspect is a low table with a record player and a box of vinyl. I recognise some of them.

"Fuck." I stare around and the enormity of their kindness hits me like a truck, straight to the gut. I lay my forearm across my stomach to squash the feeling – overwhelm, anguish, hesitancy, loss, appreciation, gratitude – I don't know what the fuck it is, but it feels like a lead ball trying to burst out. "Did you do this?" I ask turning to look back at Julie.

A dark flush spreads across her face and down her neck. "Yes," she says quietly. "We opened the space up years ago because it was so wasted. Little spooky, dark rooms," she shudders, "we hardly ever came up here because it gave us the creeps! Eventually we decided that we should do something with it, because we'd done everywhere else, and it was the last part of the castle that we'd not touched. I can't tell you how dusty it was! We had to buy thick overalls and masks just to be able to walk through the bottom door! Anyway, it took a long time to do, and was a job to do a job because we were so conscious of not earning the money we were being paid."

I wander over to the music stand and look out at the sea. *If only...*

Julie carries on talking, "We took down the walls and the windows needed replacing so Mark knocked some bricks out to make them bigger. I argued about that because it's listed, he shouldn't have done it, but he did it anyway. He figured we'd worry about permission later! I have to tell you, the trips up and down the stairs to empty all the rubbish made us more fit than we'd ever been, although if you could have heard the cracks and creaks of our knees, you'd have worn earplugs!" She laughs. "He spent all his time up here sanding, varnishing and roped me in to do the painting."

"It's incredible."

She smiles. "Well, when we found out that you owned it and that you were planning on coming up here, Mark added extra electrics under the window for your instruments. He said the view would be the best place to get inspiration for music because you can see the sea. Mark wanted you to have somewhere to work and create. He was so sad when you stopped releasing records, he's got everything you've ever released..." She falls silence and chews her lip. The small action reminds me of Molly and the ball in my gut feels heavier.

"You read the magazine?" I ask, realising.

"Yes, it was shoddy journalism if you ask me."

"I agree! The man is an arse..." I grin, "do you like rock music?"

"God, no. I'm a country fan..." she stops in horror, "no offence!"

"None taken!"

She smiles. "Mark hates my music, he's into rock, but as I said to him, it would be very dull if we all liked the same things!"

A memory of Molly singing to the boyband in the kitchen comes into my head. "It would be," I agree.

"Mark was in a band at school and I think he secretly wanted to be a rock star so turned this room into the one he would have liked it if he'd made it! It was bordering on obsession! We can change the furniture and things if you don't like them. It was all second hand that we found online. We've cleaned it up, but it may not be your taste." She closes her eyes and takes a deep breath. "We were so worried about spending money we'd not been asked to spend that we didn't think we should add new furniture to the list!"

"I'm so glad that you took the risk because it's perfect. Perfect." I look down at the polished floor and a lump forms in my throat. "it's been a long time since anyone did anything nice for me. A long, long time." I blink back unexpected tears. She doesn't say anything just pats my arm gently and I put my hand over hers. "Thank you." I say in a strangled voice, "you have no idea what this all means to me..."

"The castle will look after you, Jonny. There is only light here. We moved up here and we never looked back. Your job gave us the space to find the peace, resolution and acceptance we needed."

"Did you have something to run from too?"

"We wanted children, but it never happened. We tried to pretend it was ok, but as our friends had more and more babies we felt such a loss, delighted for them, of course, and we have lots of wonderful godchildren and nieces, nephews and so on, but even so, there was a loss that was too painful to bear. We came here before our lives splintered and we found the magic we'd been desperately needing. Now we could never imagine living anywhere else, the village and the castle is as much a part of us as we are of it." She smiles softly. "You'll find the magic here too." Julie glances at her watch. "We will leave you to settle in, unless you need anything else. The fridge and freezers are full, we didn't know what you liked so got everything we could think of. We are not far away, we can be here in five minutes, our telephone number is on the kitchen table, there is limited mobile signal up here and the castle has no Wi-Fi so it's landline, carrier pigeon or smoke signals!"

I laugh, "when I came for peace, I didn't think it would be quite so extreme!"

She grins, "you won't know yourself in a couple of days!"

"I don't know myself now!" I cross to the window and look down at the ocean. "I hope I find the magic that you did."

"You will, Jonny, you will."

***

It's really fucking peaceful. I'd expected to feel anxious and twitchy all alone in a strange building, in the middle of nowhere, but I don't. I like my own company, and I never thought I'd say it. Julie and Mark have left me alone but there is kindness everywhere I look. The fridge and freezer are bursting with home cooked meals, fruit and vegetables. Their compassion gives me a warm feeling. Like there is something good in the world, after all. I've been so used to arseholes, fair-weather friends and Freddie, who supposed to be my best friend, but no better than all the others. Out of everyone who dropped me like a fucking hot potato, he has hurt me the most. It bothers me more than I would ever admit, but being honest with myself is proving to be more healing than I'd ever realised.

I put one of the meals into the oven as instructed and throw some frozen veg into a pan. Then I pop open a beer from the cooler next to the fridge and take a swig. The beer tastes good. It's been years since I've had one, life taking me far too many times down the whiskey path to oblivion. Not anymore. I've not had a whiskey since the day before I met Molly, and I don't plan on ever having one again. But the beer, ah the beer is good, and it doesn't bring the demons with it.

I wander around the castle. It's become a daily ritual, as though daring myself to get bored with it all. I can't believe this is all mine. The hotel always felt like a noose around my neck, something to remind me of everything I lost, but the castle has begun to show me everything I earned. It's pretty fucking gross that I had so much money I could buy this and fund its care without even blinking, but I don't carry the resentment here. It doesn't weigh me down. I don't drink to find oblivion anymore, I drink because I sit out and look at the sea and reflect, not get lost in the fucking gloom. I feel different. It doesn't stop me missing Molly so much I want to rip out my own heart, but something is changing. I'm changing, and I cry. A lot.

There is always something to have me sobbing but even then, I don't hear the whiskey calling my name. There is a lot to cry about, but I don't stop the tears. Like now, walking over to the window of my bedroom and looking out at the water, tears are rolling down my face. Dunno why. They just are. Maybe because I dreamt about my mum last night and woke up unable to breathe and tangled in my sheets, sweating like a pig, or maybe because of all the shit I've done over the years. Who the fuck knows.

Perhaps I really will get it all back because there is something special inside these walls. I just pray that I will be deserving of it. I can hear Molly in my head, her kindness *it's all yours for the taking, Jonny,* and her belief that I deserve it all again. I hope I do deserve it and that the crushing musical block will somehow lift. If I'm going to find my music again, this is the place for it. I sit down in the chair beside the window and sip my beer. I needed this place. I needed the quiet. I needed my demons to stop shouting at me and for my father's voice to be silenced. *Don't forget whose son you are, boy.* I feel revulsion to even share DNA with that man - the violent, abusive poor-excuse for a man who battered my mother until she was a bloody mess and then battered her some more. *You are nothing like your father.* Oh Molly, I never thought I was but my treatment of women has been shameful. Fucking shameful. I was never going to be him, but I've copied his behaviour. I hate him. I hate him with every single fucking bit of me and I long for the day that I'm told that he is dead, because until he is I will always be *the fucking little shit who should never have been born.*

Molly

I've gotten used to being alone. Ella rings me every day if she's not had a text from me, so there is a link to the outside world and my mum is threatening to come and visit, but I've so far managed to put her off. I'm not ready for all the questions about Paul and how I ended up working for a once-famous rock star. Mum has the knack of seeing right through me so it's much easier to avoid her. She knows what I'm doing but she gets it. She's cool like that. How long I can keep her at bay, remains to be seen.

I've spent time getting to know the hotel and now that I can see it clearly, I am able to visualise how it will look. There isn't much I can do until the skips arrive, but I've begun emptying the rooms downstairs and there is a big pile of soaking bedding and table linen in the middle of the reception floor. Clearing all that was a horrible job, and the smell of mouldy material seems to be hovering around me. Still, the time has been worth it. Ideas have flooded my vision boards, which are now propped in every room, and I've put paint samples on the walls. If I think about the pressure of the job, I suddenly can't breathe and the anxiety I've been keeping at bay thunders upwards making my head spin. So, I don't think if I can help it. Yoga has been a lifesaver and I do it every day. Outside, with the view of the sea beyond, it helps me focus because otherwise I feel sure I would crumple. I try not to let Jonny into my thoughts so instead he creeps into my dreams, and I wake up feeling the loss all over again. It sucks.

I make a coffee and sit down in the library with my feet curled up under me. I spend most of my downtime in this room, well, until it gets dark, and then I head for the sanctuary of bar. The darkness is when I feel vulnerable, and if the night is still and I can hear the waves crash down onto the beach, I get caught by the grip of icy fear. So, I turn up the music, light the log burner and push the darkness away. Sometimes it works, other times the wine glass is slightly fuller.

I love the library. The books all got damaged so I can't read, but the space is still so calming that the smell of damp doesn't matter so much. The vision board for this room rests on my lap but my heart sinks when I look at it. Even though Ella loved it the most out of all the boards I've created for the hotel, I know that it's wrong. "For fucks sake," I groan, "what was I thinking?" I've tried to blend the colours with the light that comes in but all I have is an ugly clash. "I can't do this," I throw the board onto the floor and burst into tears, sobbing until I'm a drooling mess. I'm not crying about the room. I'm crying about everything else. I let the tears flow until there are no more and as I dry my face a ray of sunshine floods in through the window and rests on a gold statue.

That's why it's wrong.

There is no music in here.

I sprint from the room, along the short corridor to take the stairs two at a time to my suite. My huge artbook sits on the table with my pens and the bag of material swatches I've been working from. I grab them all into a haphazard pile and head back to the library. This room needs to inspire, there needs to be art and music as well as books. *Yes, Molly, yes!*

I lay the book on the coffee table and tip out the paint strips from the bag. I lose myself and all sense of time as I work on a new plan for the room, erasing and redoing, liberally painting a colour sample on the walls and another on the woodwork, barely stopping for a drink until the ideas blend into the perfect design. I don't believe that ever again I will design a room that is so alive. Silvery grey walls to match his eyes and darker silver fabric covering the furniture. The panelling between the book shelves will be covered with a collage made from really arty photos of Jonny I found in a vintage poster store online, framed music sheets

113

of the greats will hang on the large wall at the back of the library, alongside prints of classic novels. Everything blends beautifully with the evening sunlight that still streams in through the window. It looks exactly right. "Thank you," I whisper to the fading sun, "thank you."

I yawn and stretch my legs out straight from the chair, arms up high until my armpits feel as though they are going to split. The day has vanished, and I feel suddenly weary. I move slightly and my sluggish body creaks in protest. "Oof," I groan, as a muscle twinges in my chest. "Getting old, Moll." I put my pens into the case and bag up the material and paint cards. "That's enough for today." My stomach makes a huge growl, so I tiredly drag myself up from the chair and do a couple of yoga poses, pushing my aching body into a gentle flow, then head off to the kitchen to pop a potato into the oven. I down a glass of water but with time to kill until the potato is baked, I go for a swim.

I strip off my clothes and stand on the edge, looking down at the flat, clear water. I don't know if I'll ever be completely healed from the trauma, but I can be brave. There is a sharp, clear memory of Corey and I river jumping, laughing like lunatics and snogging in the sunshine, that unexpectedly fills my vision. My first love. I smile at the gentle reminder of the delicate sweetness of the young love, watching the images playing like a movie before my eyes. I can miss him now. There is no one to complain or criticise, nor tell me to *stop bloody crying, Moll, it was ages ago,* I can just miss him. I wonder what he would be doing with his life, what choices he would have made, I wonder if we would have stayed together, or if life would have sent us along different paths. I can still hear his laugh, the infectious giggle that would have anyone around him roaring with mirth.

"Gosh, I miss you Corey," I say looking up at the stained-glass window at the back of the chapel. "I'm so sad that you had to die." A tear rolls down my face and plops into the pool. The grief feels overwhelming after years of having to bury it, pretending it didn't exist to appease Paul's jealousy. I let the wave come, the sadness erupting out of me with feral sounds that echo around the chapel. There are no more tears just the wounded roaring of heartbroken, teenage Molly, mourning the loss of her first love, crying out to the empty room until eventually the sounds subside to a quiet whimper and the ache in my stomach clears.

I look down at the water. It's still, barely a ripple marring the surface, and now that the lights are on, the bottom of the pool is visible. There is no scary monster, or freak wave, other than what I brought in here with me. "Come on, Moll, jump." I can do this by myself, I can. The river jumping memory floats away and another comes into my mind - new, recent but just as warm - Jonny taking my hand in his soft, safe palm and saying, *"I'll jump with you. I've got you."*

Two loves, decades apart, both without the happy ending that's promised in the fairy tales and the last thought I have, as I dive down into the water, is that there is no one here to hold my hand, and it doesn't feel as though there will ever be again.

I think about the false promises that indoctrinate us as kids while I pound through the pool. The 'one true love,' the 'happily ever after,' the dreams that start with 'once upon a time,' - everything to build us up and let us down. I push myself through the water, faster and faster until the sheer effort of swimming finally quiets my furious mind and there is nothing to hear but the splashes of the water as my hands slice through. Up and down, up and down until my heart is thrashing against my ribs and I can no longer catch my breath. It's only at the moment of complete exhaustion that I feel calm. Something has shifted and I tiredly pull myself from the pool feeling cleansed.

I rub the water from my body and put my clothes back on. I can smell the baked potato wafting along the corridor and my pace quickens to the kitchen. Adding a tin of beans to a pan, and grating cheese, I assemble my dinner and take the corridor to the bar. My food doesn't last long and after I've eaten every last bean, I light the log burner. I sit with my feet up on the coffee table, listening to the music coming through the speakers and watch as the flames flicker and dance over the wood. I don't need the warmth, but the fire adds a cosiness to the room and makes me feel secure in this broken building. I understand why Jonny likes this room the best. Being in the centre of the hotel with no windows, there is safety in the cocoon.

There is no safety in the memories though, with Jonny opposite me, his wolf-eyes orange in the firelight. I wish I didn't long for him. I wish I could let him go as just a moment in time, and move into the next moment, but he's everywhere. I can feel him, smell the citrussy scent, hear his laugh - despite him hating the hotel, he is everywhere within it.

I lean back on the sofa and look around the room. It's so dreary in here. Dark pictures, the wrong lighting – it has nothing to offer outside of a storm. I drain my wine glass and put it down on the coffee table. "No time like the present, Moll." I say to myself, using the controller to turn up the music. The playlist switches to cheery pop and I dance around the room, wincing as my sore muscles complain, taking the frames down and propping them against the bar where I can look at them in detail. There is hope for some of them, a brighter coloured frame would definitely help. I walk down to Jonny's office for some blank paper, on which I scrawl 'keep' 'skip' 'charity' and stick them up in three corners of the bar. "Room by room," I tell myself. "Small bites, Moll, small!"

My tiredness evaporates. I turn the music up further until the glasses rattle against each other on the bar. I sing. I dance. I take frames down from the walls and put them into piles on the floor. I spin exuberantly out of the bar and the music pumps from every speaker in the building as I strip room after room until the bar is full of art, lamps, candelabras and ornaments. My arms ache from the loads I've carried, and my legs scream after the endless trips up and down the stairs but I'm still able to walk to the kitchen and take a gooey chocolate mousse from the fridge and pour another glass of wine. "All is not lost, Molly!"

The dessert doesn't last long but I peruse the pictures and trinkets, letting ideas float in and out of my head as I sip the wine. "Think, Molly," I mutter out loud, "think retreat, refuge, sanctuary." The ideas wash over me, and almost in a trance I stack items in each of the three corners. By the time I finish, the night has begun to give way to the day, and the clock reads five am. Wearily I climb the stairs to my room and crash out, fully clothed on the bed.

✳✳✳

"Hello, love, you Molly Bloom?" The huge man towers over me as he squints at his clipboard, beads of sweat glistening on his forehead. I watch as one plops down onto the paper.

"Yes." I nod, stifling a yawn, as he pulls out a hanky and wipes it across his head. It's boiling today and I didn't pack for a heat wave. My legs are sweating in the leggings I slept in, and there is a sweaty smell from under my armpits. What a catch! "Can I help you?"

"I'm from the skip hire company."

"I thought you were coming tomorrow." I mumble. He squints further at the forms on the clipboard.

"Nope, definitely today." He gestures to the lorry at the bottom of the driveway. "Where do you want them." He glances around the at the devastation, "or don't it matter?"

I want to correct him. "Over there -" I point to the flat area adjacent to the drive "- would be good please, not too far for me to carry stuff out."

He assesses the space. "A bit too close to the slope, don't want 'em to tip. Drive ok?"

I nod slowly, "as long as there is space for the work vans to get around the back, then yes, that's fine."

"Gotcha. Sign here please." He hands me the sweaty clipboard and yells down to the lorry driver. "Up 'ere Bri."

The lorry driver crunches the vehicle into gear, and it groans up the drive. I scan the document and sign the bottom. "Will I get a copy of this?"

The man scribbles on another form and hands it to me. "Everything is on here, including payment and all other charges. You'll get an invoice at the end of each week, that's how we do it, easy like."

"Ok, thanks and how often will it get emptied?"

"Just ring. We'll charge per empty as well as the hire per week. Not weekends though, me an' Bri don't work weekends."

"Right." I nod again and look down at the form, "thanks."

"Don't envy you love, big job you've got 'ere."

"It'll keep me out of trouble!"

"Not much trouble to get into around 'ere, love. A young thing like you should be in town. Come on then Bri," he says loudly, "let's unload and get back, I need a brew."

'Bri' pushes a lever and the springs squeal and grind as the long arm lifts each of the skips down onto the ground. The thud of the skips landing onto the tarmac sends trembles through the ground. I step back inside the doorway until all four are in place.

"Right then love, we're done. If ya need anything, ring, otherwise I'll be in touch. Don't overfill them, causes a hazard lifting them up again. 'K?"

"I won't!"

"See ya then love."

"Bye." I grin as he heaves his huge bulk up into the cab and they manoeuvre the lorry back down the drive. I close the front door and fasten the lock, grateful that it has finally been fixed and I no longer have to wriggle the desk into place. Bouncing across reception and skipping up into the bar, I select a playlist from the iPad and turn up the volume. From out of all the speakers on the ground floor come the loud sounds of the boyband play list and, singing at the top of my voice, I turn my attention to the pictures I took down yesterday. I feel excited by what I can achieve here, overwhelmed, but excited and with just over a week before the construction crews arrive, decisions have to be made. "Right then, Molly, let's get inspired."

***

The four skips gape like hungry mouths waiting for food as I begin carrying out the storm-damaged pictures and ornaments. I've kept frames that could be salvaged, and they now lie on the driveway, ready for painting. It takes no time to fill one of the skips and I head back indoors to tackle the ensuite bathrooms. Music blares as I salvage what I can and begin the painful process of taking the rest to the skips. "Why so many bloody stairs and no lift." I grumble on my tenth trip down the stairs, "surely there is a law about that." Sweat rolls down my forehead and mixes with dust, stinging my eyes. "For fucks sake," I drop everything to wipe my eyes on my tee-shirt. The sticky, wet fabric does nothing to help so I rinse my face with a flannel in one of the first-floor bathrooms. The image looking back at me in the mirror is frightful. Bright red in the face, hair on end, tee-shirt clinging uncomfortably to every stinking part of me. I look like I've just dragged myself from a furnace via a cess pit. I dry my face on a disgusting, damp-smelling hand towel and leave the bedroom. "It's just as well I'm here alone," I mutter, sniffing my armpits before picking up the discarded items and heading back down the stairs to deposit them in the skip. When I reach reception, I notice a suitcase beside the front door and a teenager looking anxiously at me from the bar steps.

"Where is my dad?" She asks thickly. "I can't find him." She chews on her bottom lip as though willing herself not to cry. "I've been ringing him, but his phone keeps going to voicemail. Has something happened? Where is everyone?"

"They had to leave when the hotel got damaged in the storm." Her face pales. Shit. "Your dad? Are you Jonny's daughter, Aria?" I ask and she nods anxiously. "Was he meant to be here?"

She nods again and bites down hard on her lip.

For fuck's sake, Jonny. I take a deep breath. "I'm so sorry, Aria, your dad isn't here. It's just me for the next couple of weeks."

"Oh, crap. I told him I was coming, I sent him the dates. He was supposed to meet me from the train." I watch Aria try to compose herself before she asks, "who are you?" She takes a step backwards and her face crumples a little more. "I've not met you before, why are you here if no one else is?" I search her face to find Jonny, but the delicate auburn-haired, green-eyed beauty has none of Jonny's features. Her mum must be stunning. Damn it.

"I'm Molly," I say, putting the trash on the reception desk. "I'm…" I pause. I have no idea what to say, *a friend of your dad's,* which isn't true, and *the decorator* makes me sound like the slutty bit on the side. She waits curiously. "I'm refurbishing the hotel." Simple. Truthful.

She looks around her, nose wrinkling. "You're really staying here? On your own? It smells disgusting."

"It really, really does!" I grin, "it doesn't matter how many times I open the windows, the smell just doesn't go away."

"What happened?"

"A huge storm happened. I've never seen anything like it before, it was terrifying. I hadn't realised it was coming so I was caught in it down by the development kitchen and practically got swept away by the sea but, someone was looking out for me that day." I say smiling, "I ended up here and lived to tell the tale."

"With my dad?"

"Yes." I feel my face begin to burn and I walk across reception to open the window, which isn't really needed as the door is wide open but anything to avoid her gaze. "If he'd not been here, I would have died."

"Oh." I can hear her mind whirring, "that must have been awful."

"The storm or your dad?"

Aria laughs, "the storm, my dad isn't so bad. Although, he forgot me. Again." She sniffs loudly.

"How did you get here?"

"I look a taxi. I thought Dad was meeting me but when he wasn't at the station, I thought he probably mixed the times up, so I just got into the first taxi outside." My face must fall because she hurriedly says, "it was fine. It was a proper taxi, and I sent a photo of the number plate and badge to my friend."

"Good thinking." I scratch my dirty head and ask, "does your mum know you're here?"

"Yes, it was all arranged because she's in America this week with my stepdad and my grandma is on a cruise. I am meant to be here for the first part of half term with dad before I go to Egypt next week for a dig..."

"A dig?"

"It's an archaeology trip."

"To Egypt?" Aria nods, "wow," I say, "our class trips were to Weston Super Mare."

"My teacher is really good."

"It sounds like it." I bob my head up and down, "look, why don't I put all this" – I gesture to the trash I brought down – "out in the skip and then I'll make you a drink and some lunch. You must be hungry after your journey?"

Aria hesitates. "I don't know what to do." She bursts into tears, "there isn't anywhere else to go. All my friends have gone away, and I can't go back to school because it's closed for two weeks. The only other person is idiot Chelsea, but I would rather sleep on a bench than go there, she hates me. I hate her."

"Aria," I say quietly, "you don't have to go anywhere. You can just stay here. I'm not a crazy, psycho person so you will be safe and, besides, the company would be nice as I'm talking way too much to myself! Leave a voicemail for your dad so he knows you're already here and I'm sure he'll call you as soon as he can. He may very well be on his way back from wherever he's been, and just got delayed. He'll probably come through the door at any moment with a flat phone battery, worried about you." *Wishful thinking there, Moll.* "The Wi-Fi is on but if you get bored with streaming tv and social media, there is loads that you could help me with, if you wanted to. I kind of feel responsible for you now, and really wouldn't feel happy if you went off somewhere and your parents didn't know."

"You're so nice," she says, wiping her eyes. "Loads nicer than idiot Chelsea."

"I'm sure she was nice." I'm fishing and I'm ashamed but like an obsessed freak, any titbit of information about how awful Chelsea is, would make me feel better.

"Oh no, she was a total bitch." Aria's tone gets brighter as she goes into a full flow. "My dad was way too good for her. Of course, the girls at school thinks she's amazing because she's always seen with the right people, wearing the right stuff, but God, it was so embarrassing that my stepmother was posting pictures with everything hanging out and sprawled over some rich man. I hate her. Hate. Her. She is evil. Even when Dad was losing all the houses and cars, you know, everything he worked for, she just didn't care. She kept spending and moaned all the time about how miserable her life was and how it was all Dad's fault. She used to go into savage rages because sometimes he had to cut her credit cards up, but he still kept paying for me to be at a brilliant boarding school. She thought I should go to the secondary school in our area. She used to argue with Dad about it all the time. Honestly, you've never met a more horrible person. My dad is so much better than her. I kept telling him to divorce her, and find someone nice, but he didn't. Although now he has finally dumped her. Thank God. Even my mum is happy about it, and she never says anything about Dad's love life, even when he married Chelsea who was the most idiotic of all his bimbo girlfriends. Chelsea was always really rude to my mum, probably because she was jealous that my mum is beautiful and clever and amazing. Chelsea is just dumb.

"They've split up?"

"Who, my mum and dad? That was ages ago!"

"No, your dad and his wife."

"Yeah, a few weeks ago. It was like he had an epiphany - I love that word, I use it all the time even though my teachers keep telling me to find a new word. *Aria, you can't use epiphany three times in one paragraph, Aria, find a word that means the same but isn't epiphany,* they just go on at me, but I use it anyway. It's a great word. Anyway, my dad had one, and he dumped her. I was so happy. He even sounded happy when he told me, and my dad hasn't been happy since he married her. It was a good day, that day."

"Hmmm." I comment, feeling my heart skipping, back-flipping and all-round disco-dancing in my chest. He's left her. Does that mean the kiss meant something to him, after all? I try to squash the rapidly rising hope that maybe he does feel the same way as I do. I was so convinced he did, but the rejection...damn that stung.

"Molly?"

"Yeah?"

"Why has your face gone all red, are you alright? Are you having a heart attack or something? It's fine if you are, I did first aid at school..."

"No, I'm not having a heart attack. I'm ok." *Liar, liar pants on fire.* I ignore the bubbles in my belly and pick up the trash, coughing as the dust clouds up into my face. "I'll just put this out and then we'll eat. Do you want to take your bags up?"

"Where shall I stay? Dad's suite?"

I nod, "it's probably the best room, all the rest are damp."

"Ok."

Aria pulls the handle of her suitcase towards the bottom of the stairs. "It's about time Dad got a lift."

I laugh, "The exact same thing crossed my mind too!"

"I think I'm going to like staying here with you."

"That's nice to know, I think I'm going to like you staying here."

Aria bumps her case up the stairs, and I take the rubbish out to the skip. So, Jonny has left his wife. Suddenly the world seems infinitely brighter and a smile spreads across my face. Ok, universe, you have my attention.

Jonny

The sunlight blazing in through the open windows of my bedroom rouses me from a dream I was having where I was on stage. Alone. No band supporting me. Singing the song that will forever be Molly's boyband song, to a crowd who were making no sound, just holding lights out as though a million stars were in the stadium, all shining for me. Surprisingly, I don't feel the usual grip of self-revulsion as I ordinarily do after a dream of the lost stardom, instead, I feel hopeful. Proper sleep has evaded me for decades, and in the recent years, I have just passed out at the bottom of a whiskey bottle, but last night, something changed. In the silence and solitude of the castle on the island, there was an energy shift, and I slept.

It feels significant.

Really fucking significant.

I glance at the cheap watch on my wrist. I bought it in Glasgow when I arrived. It's non-descript and nothing like the ostentation diamond watches that I used to have. Back in the day. When I was someone. I realise how little I mind the cheap watch. I wait for the *how the mighty have fallen* rhetoric to come but the voice is mute. How long has it been since the voices were silent? I look again. Fuck me, I've been in bed for sixteen hours. Sixteen! I laugh. It's a belly laugh that shakes my body from the tips of my toes to the top of my head. The last time I was in a bed for sixteen hours, I wasn't sleeping, and I definitely wasn't alone. I'm not sure I'd swap the mirth I'm feeling right now for a sixteen-hour romp. Then I pull a face. "Who are you kidding, Jonny? You're not dead yet!" I yawn widely and stretch out under the duvet. I don't know what time I fell asleep, but I remember how peaceful it was to be lying in the darkness, staring out at the stars as they twinkled a myriad of colours and wondering if

Molly was looking at the same sky. It was so tranquil that I must have just drifted off.

This castle is fucking awesome.

I yawn again and roll over to face the window. The ocean outside is so still that it looks like a painting. Not a cloud mars the bright blue of the sky, and overhead the soaring sea birds, call out to one another. Probably saying *have you seen that crazy fucker lying in bed laughing like a dick!* Ah, they can say what they like, maybe it's time to stop worrying what people, and sea birds, think about me. I've spent all my life trying to make people like me, to give a shit about me, to think I'm important and that I'm better than everyone else. My ambition blinded me to the pitfalls and the reality was that superstardom was probably just to prove to my dad that I was more than a *fucking snivelling little bastard who deserves a fucking good beating.*

Fuck him.

He can't hurt me here. I'm safer than I've ever been before in this castle on the island. I can't remember the last time I felt like this. *Yes, you can! When you were with Molly,* the voice says, *you were safe with her.* Yes, I was. I was safe enough to tell the truth, to admit things that I'd never even admitted to myself. I was safe enough to completely crumble because she was there to pick me up. I was safe when I kissed her until all the feelings I had fucking terrified me and I pushed her away.

Have I ever not been scared? For years after Mum and I escaped my abusive father I used to wake up in a cold sweat, often having wet the bed because I was so petrified that he would find us. I didn't go to sleep sober for decades. Until Molly. I could breathe for the first time with her around.

That sort of fear isn't easily overcome not even with all the security I had and the huge gates that kept out the world. When Aria was born, the fear heightened, and even though I promised her I would always protect her and that I would never be the sort of father that I had, I broke the promise. I got wasted and the fear was buried under the excesses. I've let her down time and time again but this time, when I promise to be a great father, I will be.

I set a reminder on my phone to call her about coming to Scotland for half term instead of Cornwall - which will have to wait for when I finally get a signal - and roll myself over to the other side, sliding out of bed. Aria will love it here, despite her protestations at being a cool city chick. I can't wait to see her for the holidays, it will be the first one that I have been fully present for. I grin and stretch dramatically.

Pulling a sweatshirt over my bare torso, I take the stairs down to the kitchen, trying to put Molly out of my mind. I put the coffee on to percolate and shove my feet into the discarded trainers under the table. I jog up the few steps to the front door and slide back the locks, stepping out into the bright sunshine and walk along to the bridge.

There is nothing around me but ocean on three sides and an expanse of green that runs along the coastline for as far as I can see. In the distance rolling hills stand tall against the backdrop of blue sky. The castle is the only building in the area and I'm still wondering who chose to put it somewhere so remote. Some miserable fucker who hates the world probably. It's the perfect place to be angry, stuck out on a rock separated from the land by the sea, at least until the bridge was put in. The bridge is a brighter stone than the castle and the carvings on it are sharper, newer. I run my hand along the stone. Then I laugh, stroking stone, admiring views, gazing at oceans...what the fuck happened to me? Jonny Raven, once a stroker of women, admirer of big breasted blondes and gazer at hot slutty types making out with each other for my titillation has become – actually, I don't know what I've become. Until recently I was nothing but a sad, lonely, wasted, broke drunk, the scars on my stomach are a recent reminder of how bad that got. Now? I don't know

127

and it feels strangely ok not to know. I take a long breath in and expel it slowly. Perhaps there is something to be said for Molly's suggestion of meditation. Isn't that what all the rock stars are doing these days? From the images I see online, no one is into sex, drugs or rock and roll anymore, it's all green juices and yoga.

Fuck that shit.

I follow the wall around the castle. There isn't a garden, but at the back of the building is a huge, paved area that looks out over the sea. Julie and Mark have put outdoor furniture in place, sofas around a large glass table with a fancy fire pit in the centre. It's all too big for one person. Still, it's another place to sit and stare at the endlessness while I find myself. Find myself, who am I fucking kidding? I want to find my music, not myself. I know where I am. Here. In a castle I have no knowledge of buying, looked after by two people I had no idea that I employed, who have access to money I didn't know I parted with. I should be finding money, not myself.

I watch the tiny ripples on the surface of the water and feel a sense of calm come over me. This ever-changing vision is not something to get bored with, no matter how may days I waste time watching it. It's not stagnant, but always moving, and it seems that there is lesson in it, maybe the ocean has something to tell me. Oh, who the fuck knows. I've been alone too long and I'm trying to make sense of shit that may not have any sense to it anyway. My entire life has been created on situations that haven't made sense. I just used excess to bury it all – I got laid, got drunk, got rich, got poor and was nearly suffocated by my own shame.

Where would I be now if Molly hadn't pulled me out of the blackness?

Dead probably. The isolation in the storm wouldn't have got me sober, regardless of my determination. I would have succumbed to the whiskey eventually and would never have known that I had this place, an investment that gave me some money and that my music was back on the radio. I would have missed it all. I would have left Aria the worst way possible, and I would only ever have been her fuck-up of a dad. Molly saved my life. She fucking saved everything.

I just hope she forgives me.

I walk around the side of the castle and back in. I can smell the coffee and take the stairs down to the kitchen two at a time, pouring a cup and drink it waiting for the toaster to pop. Liberally buttering the toast I sit down at the table and listen to the silence. I'm surprised that underneath the silence is a vibration. An energy. It's barely audible but it's there. And, just like that, my fingertips tap out a rhythm. Fuck me, I have rhythm.

I drop the coffee cup onto the table where it spills over the toast. I barely notice. All I can see is the white light. A spotlight. It's fleeting but I see it and the music...I can just about hear it if I strain hard enough. I can't reach the melody because a moment later it's gone. Tears roll down my cheeks and for the first time in years, I have the flickering faith that I just may be worthy and it just may come back.

Fuck me, it just may come back.

***

It's begun to rain, and the dark sky has turned the ocean a steel grey. Fat raindrops plop down and I'm tempted to just sit out in it. It's not cold and there is hint of blue over the mountains, *for fucks sake Jonny, have you heard yourself!* I scoop up the plate of lunch and the book I've been reading and head back inside, up to the lower landing where there are four reception rooms – library, snug, study and the wood-panelled lounge. The lounge reminds me of a bar in Camden I used to go to when I was fed up with having people around me all the time. It was the sort of bar that wasn't accidentally

129

stumbled across so when things got crazy it gave me somewhere to escape to. I sit down in the armchair and put my feet up on the table, balancing my food on my lap. Little John Jones, king of the fucking castle. If the haters could see me now.

For some reason Freddie pops into my head. I can imagine his puffy face flushing, the fleshy mouth gaping open as he looks at me and says, *what the fuck Jon, you bought a fucking castle...*and then make some comment about parties and women and all the usual shit we did back in the day. I honestly thought we were friends, but I was just a cash cow to him, like I was for everyone else. I was too drunk, or too high, too shagged or touring to notice.

I don't want to think about Freddie. It's a pain I don't need to deal with today. *Put the music on,* the voice whispers and my eyes send an involuntary glance to the CD player that sits on a tall table in the corner of the room. CD player? I laugh. Holy fuck the nineties are back! Music would cover the silence, but I don't even know what I would want to listen to. What do I like these days? I heave myself out of the chair and cross the room. There is a selection of CDs in the drawer of the table. Most of them are my albums. I feel the rush of breath as my body expels it from my lungs. The room swims and I have to grab the table to stop myself falling backwards. I wasn't expecting that. Fuck. *Just breathe*, the voice says, and I do, deep breaths, one after the other until the room comes into focus.

I can hear Molly's soft voice urging me to put one on. There is the taste of blood in my mouth as I chew down on my lower lip, reaching for one of the discs and taking it from the drawer. My second album. The one that catapulted me to fame. Tears fall and I can't wipe them away because two hands are gripped around the CD box. I end up sobbing and curled in a ball on the floor. Once more I'm little John Jones broken into pieces, bruised and bloodied, because he made a mistake.

I'm not sure how long I'm on the floor for but the tears have tried on my face, leaving my skin sticky. My hair is damp from the tears that pooled on the floor, and I'm wrapped around the CD as though it is a comfort blanket. I wait for the demons to call me a pussy, but no insults come. There is just silence. Eventually I struggle up to standing and look down at the CD in my hand. "Come on Jonny, you can do this," I whisper and put the disc into the machine. From out of the speakers comes my voice. I remember every description of my singing over the years - Husky, gravelly, growly, like vocal cords bathed in vintage whiskey, a voice to fuck to - but none of them fit how it sounds to me today. It sounds rich, pure, unique and the hairs on the back of my neck stand up. Is this what I've been hiding from for five years? This sound? How have I never heard it like this before? I sit back down in the armchair and stare out of the window at the rain, listening to my songs and I cry again. I fucking bawl like a baby who's lost his favourite toy, but I keep listening. It's a step forwards, no matter how painful it feels, and hearing my music is a monumental leap away from the fucked-up wreck I've been. So, I close my eyes and I listen. There is something. It's there and it's waiting for me. I try to grasp it but it's just too far to reach. "I'm coming," I whisper, "I'm coming for you."

***

Molly

Aria is the sweetest girl. Chatty, funny and happy to get stuck into all the worst jobs. Between us we have completely emptied the bathrooms of damp, mouldy face cloths, towels and bath mats. What was salvageable is now in the various washing machines in the hotel and everything else is in the skip. It was an unforgiving job in the heat and with sweat pouring from us, we have earned the ice creams we are now eating on the front lawn, or what's left of it, at least. The sun is blazing down so fiercely that I had to give in and wear a pair of Jonny's shorts instead of my leggings. I didn't want to go into his suite and smell his scent, but it was either that or have heatstroke, and with a minor to be responsible for, heatstroke was out.

"I tried Dad again," she says licking the melting ice cream from the cone, "and it went straight to voicemail like every other time. I hope he's alright. I wondered if I should ring the police, or something."

I look at her as she stares at the sea. "I'm sure he's fine, Aria. It's likely he's lost his phone or doesn't have a charger. I'm sure he'll call as soon as he can." I try and be upbeat but in recent days I've been just as concerned about him as her. "Have you spoken to your mum?"

"No, I've been deliberately missing her calls because she'd go nuts if she knew Dad wasn't here. He drives her mad most of the time, although they get on very well, it's just that Mum thinks he's a bit unreliable."

I say nothing.

"I just send her a message like *sorry I missed you mum, I'm having fun* because I am and you're really nice. So much nicer than bitch Chelsea."

"Thanks," I laugh, "I'm glad you think so! But, Aria, you should tell your mum the truth. If I was her, I'd want to know."

132

"She'll lose her shit."

"She may, but also remember that you're here with a total stranger, and even if your mum is in America and can't get back, she needs to know that you're being looked after. I really think you should tell her."

"I haven't lied to her," Aria says quickly, "I wouldn't do that."

"No, you haven't but you've been economical with the truth."

"Yeah, you're right. I'll ring her later." Aria bites off the top of her ice cream. "Do you miss him?"

"Who?"

"My dad?"

"I don't really know him."

Aria squints at me. "I know I'm only fifteen but I'm doing psychology and you are psychology one oh one."

"How so?" I feel my face begin to burn under her inquisitive stare.

"You go bright red every time I mention him."

"Do I?"

"Every time!" Aria grins, "it's fine, most of the girls at school have a crush on him, which I hate because they say cringy things that I really don't want to hear although, it's definitely worse that they all love idiot Chelsea. You should see them lining their lips and painting on bright red gloss like she does. Urgh," Aria shudders, "my dad has the worst taste in women, but she was the total worst. I hate her, she's like…awful. I was so embarrassed all the time because Bitchy Bonnie got to me at breakfast every single day with some shitty comment about Chelsea being prettier than me, or being half naked and snogging someone who wasn't my dad. It may be better now they've split up. I hope it is, otherwise, it won't be long before Miss Trainer, that's my PE teacher, can you imagine a more better name for a PE teacher than Miss Trainer-" she doesn't wait for me to answer, "notices that I'm

133

always accidentally-on-purpose whacking her shins with my hockey stick. Being a teenager sucks." Aria crunches her cone, "you're lovely though, I would be very happy if you dated my dad."

"I don't think that's on the cards though, Aria."

"Shame, you'd be good for him." She pops the last bit of cone into her mouth. "Was there any romance while you were hiding from the storm."

I think about the kiss, The One Perfect Moment as I've taken to calling it. The moment when I finally fit completely with someone and how I could never have let go of him. "No, nothing. We were just two people thrown together by chance and we became friends, but I had a boyfriend, he had Chelsea and it was never going to be more than that. I liked him, we laughed a lot but sorry to disappoint you, Aria, there wasn't a romance."

"Bummer." She says, lying back onto the tiny patch of grass that still remains. "That really is disappointing. So, what's next on the plan for today?"

"Well, while the weather is good, I want to paint the frames," I point to the ones lying at the back of the driveway. "I want them all to be the same colour and then decide what prints to put back in. How are your painting skills?"

"Good, I love art."

"Excellent!" I finish my ice cream. "I'll go and get the paints and you can ring your mum."

"Oh, really?"

"Yes, really. She needs to know and also, you need to let me have the travel information for Egypt so I can make sure you don't miss the plane!"

"You'll take me all the way to London."

"Sure," I smile, "that's what friends do."

I walk back inside the hotel and leave Aria to her phone call. She's a great kid and her being here is a welcome distraction from my inner monologue who doesn't shut up

134

about Jonny. The paint is stacked in reception, delivered early this morning. I pick up two tins and clamp brushes under my armpits. Something methodical like painting may just help me focus on something other than Jonny. When I get back outside Aria is looking upset.

"Mum went mad. I've never heard her be so angry. I tried to explain but she was on about calling the police and social services. I could hear Luke in the background telling her to calm down, but she is properly mad. She is ringing back to speak to you once she's called Dad." She bursts into tears. "I think I've made everything worse. What if she stops me seeing him? I don't see him that much as it is."

I put my arm around her slender shoulder. "She's just worried, and she's right to be, your dad was meant to be here, and she has no idea who I am. I'll have a chat with her when she rings, and we'll get it all sorted. Don't worry."

"But Dad..."

"Has messed up, but maybe he just got the week wrong? Maybe he's in a bad signal area, who knows, but people make mistakes and ordinarily he would have been here, because the hotel would have been open. It's just an unfortunate situation that the building flooded." I squeeze her shoulder and drop my arm, "come on Aria, wipe the tears and let's make these frames look good. Then we can decide which pictures to put where in the hotel, that will be fun."

"Ok," she sniffs and takes a brush from me. Her phone rings and I brace myself, *oh hell, Jonny of all the weeks to go AWOL.* "It's Mum for you." Aria hands me the phone and takes herself and a pot of paint across the drive to the frames. I watch her sit down and pop the paint open before I hold the phone up to my ear.

"Hello, Molly speaking."

Aria's mum, Susie speaks in a tone so filled with panic and distress that I want to cry for her. I let her say everything she needs to and then I tell her about myself, why I'm at the hotel, where I've come from and how I know Jonny. The call switches to video and we properly introduce ourselves. I notice her likeness to Aria despite the puffy, red eyes from crying. As the conversation continues, she begins to relax and by the end we're chatting like old friends. I feel a knot I didn't realise I had in my stomach, uncurl. Phew.

"Are you sure you're happy to take Aria all the way to Heathrow? It's miles."

"It will be a good break from the smell of mould," I laugh. "Honestly, it's fine, she's a great kid and she's being really helpful. It's the least I can do for all the free labour!"

Susie falls silent for a moment. "I really will kill Jonny," she says eventually. "He's always been disorganised, particularly since he stopped performing, but this is the worst thing he's ever done. I left him a voicemail but it's unlikely he'll ring me back!" She grins, "he needs someone to look after him, he doesn't do so well on his own. Mind you, he didn't do so well with that bloody bimbo either. I wasn't at all upset when Aria said they'd split up. No," Susie sighs, "he needs a decent person who won't put up with his shit but will make sure he eats properly and stops drinking so much. The trouble with Jonny is that it's hard to stay mad with him, he just has to flash those eyes…"

"I think he just needs to find his voice again." I say and she looks at me with questions on her face.

"Yeah, you're right about that. It was a tragedy when he stopped singing. I asked him why over and over, but he just said, I don't want to do it anymore. The thing is, when you've known Jonny as long as I have, you know that isn't true. He was nothing without music, it's his identity. Oh, I don't know…" she shrugs, "he's a law unto himself. Anyway, I guess I'd better go, it's dawn here and I've got a wives' brunch, I can't turn up with these bags! Lovely to meet you Molly and thanks for looking after Aria, I'm grateful that you were there."

"No worries, and enjoy your wives' brunch, sounds fun." I lie lightly. It sounds horrific.

"Fun isn't the word I'd use," Susie grimaces, "but they serve gin, so I'll survive."

We exchange goodbyes and I cancel the call. "It's all ok," I say walking over to Aria, "your mum is savage with your dad, but now she knows I'm not dodgy she's happier."

Aria visibly relaxes.

"You're doing a great job with that frame," I sit down beside her, "Let's see how many we can do then I reckon we go into town for pizza, what do you think?"

"I love pizza!"

"I love pizza too, and I especially love not cooking!"

"I like being here with you Molly."

"I like you being here too." I dip the brush into the paint. "You're making this week very cheery."

"You're so nice, I wish you could get together with my dad." She says, painting white onto the next frame.

Me too, kid, me too.

***

I wake up early. Clouds hang in the sky and the sun doesn't have the same golden glare as it did yesterday. I throw the covers back and immediately wish I hadn't. There is a chill in the air and my thin pyjamas are not enough to keep me warm. I reach for Jonny's hoodie and shrug in on, and, slipping my feet into my trainers, I groggily leave my suite. I pause outside Jonny's door but there are no sounds that suggest Aria is awake, so I make my way downstairs, wrinkling my nose against the smell in the hall. I open the window despite the chill and let the sea air in. From my position on the hill, I can hear the soft rolling of the waves onto the sand, and I feel a pull to the ocean. Checking the hoodie pocket for my phone, I walk out into the cool morning and follow the driveway down to the front. The ocean is a grey-blue, but there is no power in the waves, not yet at least. The wind has picked up a little and I pull the hood up, before crunching my way along the sand in the direction of the development kitchen. I've always loved the beach, well until the sea tried to kill me, and then I surprise myself and run headlong into the ocean, gasping at the biting chill of the water until I fall forwards and am covered by the next wave.

There is fear. For a second, a minute, a lifetime – who knows how long, I am truly petrified, but then I rise to the surface and turn onto my back, kicking my legs to stop my wet clothes pulling me down again, watching the sky as the clouds drift overhead. It's peaceful. If anyone could see me now, they'd think I had gone mad, but as I'm floating my mind is quiet. Calm. Jonny doesn't intrude on the nothingness. When I finally leave the sea for the walk back to the hotel, I feel different – stronger, focused, more self-aware and no longer afraid.

What will be, will be.

I drip up the hill and by the time I get to the front door I'm freezing cold. Stripping everything off, I run up the stairs to the shower, hoping that I don't bump into Aria on the way. Two more days with her, and three days before the construction team come and all hell breaks loose. From damp to dust – it sounds like a stepford wife horror movie. I scrub my skin free of salt water and change into clean clothes before bouncing back down the stairs in search of breakfast. Something has shifted. I feel different. I like this new feeling and I turn up the radio on the kitchen counter and sing at the top of my lungs.

By the time Aria gets up I've laid out breakfast for her and am out on the driveway painting the frames. They look so much better in a white and I'm glad I made the decision to salvage them.

"Hi Molly," Aria says sitting down beside me with a cup of tea. "I made you a drink." She hands me the mug and I take it smiling.

"Thanks, I needed this!"

"You're nearly done." She says, picking up a brush and one of the final frames, "they look really good."

"They do. We've made a good team." I test the frames we did yesterday and am pleased to find them dry. "Now we have to decide what prints we like and what will look good where."

"That sounds like fun," she says, "then what? Do we put them back up?"

"No, the team are coming to strip all the walls and take out all the carpets so nothing can go anywhere until the rooms are redecorated. These will have to be stored in the chapel, it's the only place that didn't get damaged."

"I'll be so glad to visit again without the smell!" Her phone rings and she puts the brush down to answer it. "Dad? Oh my God, Dad, where are you?"

I freeze and don't dare breathe as I try to listen to the voice on the other end.

"You're where?" She listens, her face screwing up. "Scotland? Why are you there?" Jonny is saying something to Aria, but I can't make out the words. "Oh my God Dad, you were meant to be here." He speaks back to her, and she replies with, "of course I'm fine, Dad, I'm with Molly and she's looking after me. Someone has to." I want to rip the phone from her hands and tell him that I miss him, and I want him and all the things I shouldn't ever utter out loud but instead I sit frozen to the spot. So, he's in Scotland, at the castle I found, I expect.

I try and picture what the castle would look like, would it be massive and grey, sitting on a hill with cannons poised, or small and ruinous, a little like here? I drink my tea and try not to listen anymore, but Aria's voice has gone up an octave and it's hard to shut my ears. "No, Dad don't bother. I'm cross with you, and it'll spoil my time with Molly and she's lovely." She grins at me, and her voice returns to its normal pitch. "You probably know that though. She'd be the perfect girl for you, sorry Molly…" She laughs, "Molly has just gone bright red Dad, but she said there was no romance. I think she might fancy you a bit!"

"Aria!" I say sharply, heat rising on my face, "that's enough."

"Sorry, Molly, I was only playing. Anyway, Dad, Molly is going to take me to the airport, seeing how both my parents are elsewhere. It's a miracle I'm so normal."

I stand up and walk across the drive to the back door and put my cup in the sink. He's safe. I know where he is, but it doesn't stop me wishing with all my being that he was here.

Jonny

I hang up the call, reeling. Shit. Why didn't I check the fucking term dates before I travelled to the ends of the earth? The enormity of my mistake sends chills around my body. What if Molly hadn't been there? Goddamn me to hell, I don't deserve to be a father. The next voicemail is from Aria, and the next, and the next until I get Susie's. She doesn't hold back. I slow my pace along the coastal path, town is just a few hundred yards away and I really don't want anyone to overhear the furious chastising from my ex-wife. She's right. Every word of it. I've fucked up massively and I deserve everything she says, but even so, I'd rather it was just me that listened. There's no hiding, I'll have to ring her back.

It goes to voicemail.

Thank fuck.

I leave a long message, apologising, explaining, asking for forgiveness and I hope it's enough to placate her. Susie has been the greatest possible ex but even her patience with me will only go so far, and I left our daughter at risk. Monumental risk. I thank the heavens for Molly, once again saving my arse. What on earth must she be thinking about me now? It was bad enough that I did what I did to her, but to forget entirely about my child.

"Fuuuuuuuuck," I shout across the sea and ball my hands into fists, pressing them into my eyes as though shutting out the glorious day will make it all fucking better. Of course, it won't. I've screwed up. The demons begin their vitriolic whispers, but I ignore them, I don't need to be told, I know everything they want to say.

I watch the white tipped waves roll against the rocks for the longest time, and eventually continue my way into the small town. It's quaint, with old bricked buildings lining the small cobbled high street. I pass the post office, the pub and the little shop, the greengrocers and the butchers, all decorated

141

with bunting and hanging baskets. Molly would love it. Then I stop myself, I can't keep thinking about her otherwise I'll end up taking the first train home. I'm not ready to go home. Besides, I'm not sure I will ever be able to call the hotel home. Even so, Aria's voice rings in my ears *I think she might fancy you a bit.* I grin. I can imagine the colour of Molly's cheeks and the hands that would rake through her crop of chestnut hair. She may well do, kiddo, but not nearly as much as I fancy her.

Beyond the main street are clusters of cottages, and along the harbourside are houses painted all the colours. It's chocolate box pretty, and surprisingly busy for somewhere so small. I feel the eyes on me, scrutinising the arrival of a stranger, and one as scruffy as me, so I smile and nod in greeting. I come to the small tea-shop at the end of the main street, with iron tables and chairs set out on the cobbles, and go inside.

The waitress looks up and me and smiles. "Good morning," she says, "take a seat, I'll be right with you." Her accent is gentle and lilting, the inflections flowing into each other like a wave. A rhythm. She's pretty too, and old enough that if this was a few years ago, I would have fucked her and left her for the next willing victim. Not today. Not ever again.

"Thanks." I smile back at her and sit down at a table in the window. I open the laptop in my rucksack and log into the Wi-Fi from the password chalked on a board at the counter. I check my emails, mostly from Tom Masters telling me what Molly is wasting my money on, which turns out to be so insignificant that I feel a rage towards him for being a dick. I fire back an email telling him as much, then move onto an email from Jim Hartell. The waitress comes over and I order a coffee and slice of cake, before turning my attention back to the email. Bloody Chelsea and her demands. I raise my settlement offer to include a one-bed flat in London, but that's it. She can't have any more.

Then I do the unthinkable. I google myself. I used to do it all the time back in the day, usually after a few too many whiskeys, but sober and in a café, if feels a little ridiculous. It doesn't stop me though and I sit up straighter and straighter as I find comments about me on music review sites. Good comments. Awesome comments. Fucking mind-blowing comments from kids just discovering me, kids who want to be me, young bands covering my music. A lone tear falls onto the checked tablecloth and the waitress looks at me quizzically as she places my coffee and cake down.

"Are you alright?"

"Yes, fine, thank you." I want to tell her that I'm more than alright, but I hold back. It's a small town, and I don't want the people here thinking I'm insane. I turn my attention back to the screen.

My music is back on the scene! No fucking way. I thought it was just the one song, but the shitty magazine article has hit a whole new generation and they're all talking about me. I pour milk into the coffee and then change the browser search. It's the ego boost I needed. *He's so hot – what I would do to him – those eyes – Jonny Raven? Jonny Ravishing, more like – I'd sell my husband and kids for one night with him* - streams of comments that make me grin. *Where is Jonny? Is he making new music? Is he touring again?* Endless questions that fill my soul with a bright, white light. I make a mental note to send the shitty journalist a crate of whiskey and a stripper. That feels like a suitably 'rock star' gift, from someone who faded and came back because of him.

Ego stoked, I then have a look at the rock charts. I used to pay close attention, but once the crash came, I stopped looking. My mouth falls open. There I am. In the top twenty. Two songs. My two favourites as it happens, there in black and white on the music streaming sites. A wave of emotion comes thundering down on me, and I drown in it. I must have made a sound because the waitress, and a couple I didn't see come in, look over at me and I smile, embarrassed. For a moment I am higher than high, floating above myself, until I remember that there is nothing new. I have nothing new to give, and the feelings of elation drift away. Fuck.

I check the bank, pay Aria's outstanding school fees, put some money in her account and settle a couple of bills. It's nice to see that the account barely takes a hit from the spending. How long has it been since I didn't have to count every penny? I arrange a car to take Aria to the airport with a return trip for Molly, and email Aria and Susie the information. Finally, I order a huge bouquet of flowers to be sent to Molly, with a thank you note. *You should give them to her yourself.* Yes, I should but if I go back now, I won't be anything other than a quitter, and she deserves better than that.

"Excuse me?" I look up at a teenager standing nervously beside my table. He hands a piece of paper to me and says, "can I have your autograph please?" I look behind him to a group of lads with mugs of hot chocolate in front of them, all looking at me with disbelief on their faces.

"You know me?" I ask, taking the paper.

"Yes, you're Jonny Raven. My dad says you're a total legend. I've...we've...been listening to your songs. We are covering one at the barn dance next month, you should come...not that we're any good," he says quickly, "not like you, you'll probably be really annoyed by how bad we are, but we're big fans now...our girlfriends think we're good."

"Tell you what," I say, scrawling my name on the paper. "If your girlfriends think you're good, then that's good enough for me. Just tell me where I need to be, and I'll be there."

"Really?" He breathes, "you'll really come?"

"Sure." His friends nudge each other, grins spreading over their faces. This feels fucking amazing. He writes the address down on a napkin and I put it in my wallet. "Which song are you covering?"

"Time."

"Good choice, tricky chord change in the middle."

"Yeah, I keep messing it up."

"Want some help?" I ask casually.

"From you?" he gasps, looking over to his mates and back at me.

"Why not? I wrote it!" I grin. "I'm living in the castle, come there tomorrow. Eleven-ish. Let's see what you can do."

"All of us?"

"Well, the band, not the entire town." I close my laptop and pack it away in the bag. "You know where the castle is, I take it?"

"Yes."

"Good." I stand up from the chair and go to the counter to pay my bill. I pay the kids' bill too and leave the café to walk down by the harbour. What has happened to me? I hate scenery and shit, but the energy is different here, I'm different here and the kids' band has suddenly given me a purpose.

I really fucking hope they're not shit.

I didn't think about that.

What do I do if they are?

Fuck.

***

The bell goes bang on eleven and I open the door to five slightly terrified looking teenagers, three of whom have guitars slung over their shoulders.

"Morning lads," I say jovially, "stop looking so nervous and come in. I assume your parents know you're here?"

"Yes," the one I spoke to yesterday says. "My mum wanted to come and chaperone, but I said no."

"Oh, did she?"

"She fancies you," one of the others says, "that's why. Nothing to do with our safety!"

I laugh, "not everyone has taste." I usher them in and down the steps to the kitchen. "I was just making a coffee. Do you want a drink before we start?" They all nod, "and, I guess you'd better introduce yourselves, as I'm at a disadvantage because you know who I am."

"I can't believe we're here." I look at the lad who speaks with awe in his voice. "I'm Jed."

"Kyle."

"Billy."

"Ben."

"Taylor," the autograph hunter says. "Thanks for having us here."

"My pleasure." I pour out glasses of squash and hand them round. "I'm interested to see what you do with the song. Follow me, we'll go up to the lounge." The attic would be the right place really, but I can't bring myself to take them up there. *The first person to play up there has to be you.* They form a line behind me, and I take them up the two flights to the panelled lounge.

"How do you have a castle?" Jed asks, leaning out of the window. "I thought this place was empty."

"It was but now I'm here. I have a castle because I worked hard and bought it." No point telling them I was shitfaced and had no idea, it would ruin the illusion, or perhaps the truth would make me seem more like a rock star.

"Cool." He says. "Not sure what Ben is going to do, he's the drummer."

Ben sighs out a big breath. "Nothing."

"I don't have any drums here, I'm afraid, but if you go to the kitchen and get all the pans, and the wooden spoons, they'll do for banging out the rhythm at least." Ben looks quizzically at me. "When I started out, I had a battered, old guitar that had a string missing, you can improvise!" He grins, nodding, and disappears out the door. When he comes back up the other lads have arranged themselves in a formation and are making a great show of tuning their instruments.

"Who sings?"

"Me," Billy says, "I can't read music."

"Can you sing?"

"I think so."

I bet his mum has told him he can sing then it occurs to me that I may be almost feeling jealous. I feel a tingle in my fingers and a tightness in my chest. Would the teenage me have hesitated like they are? I sit with the thought. No, never. I was always going to be someone, and it was never going to be John fucking Jones. I take a few deeps breaths before I speak.

"Ok, when you're ready then let's see what you can do." They look green as I sit down in the arm chair and attempt to look like the rock star I used to be. I'm not sure I carry it off, but they take an age to play so I may be doing it better than I thought. "Come on lads, no point being here if you're not going to play a note!" No one does anything. "If you can't play in front of one person, how are you going to play in front of everyone at the barn dance? What's the most people you've played to?"

"Just a few. Our mums and our girlfriends." Taylor says.

"Ok..." I nod slowly wondering if I've completely lost my mind. "Well, I'm just one, so that's even easier."

"It's your song," he mutters.

"It's your interpretation. The great thing about music is that you can make it be whatever you want, even songs you've not written yourself. *Time* was written twenty years ago, music has changed since then, so your version is likely to

147

be more current than mine." I drink my coffee and wait for them to start. The young kid on the drums – saucepans – bangs the wooden spoons together two or three times before anyone else starts playing. I give up the rock star slouch and sit up, waiting.

Taylor turns to the three lads beside him and nods, "we've got to do this. Count us again, Ben."

"One...two...three...four," Ben says cracking the spoons together. I stifle a smile.

After a couple of dodgy starts they get into the flow and the song comes to life. Billy has a good voice, cracking where his voice isn't quite developed, but he can hold a tune. The song sounds softer with his young vocals but despite the nerves he does it justice. The three guitarists are in time with each other, but the tuning is wrong. I stop them.

"You need to tune up." I say, reaching for the nearest guitar, "you're all slightly off." Then I freeze. My hand is wrapped around the neck and the yearning to play it is taking my breath away.

"Are you alright Mr Raven, you've gone very pale." Jed takes the guitar from me and someone hands me a glass of squash.

"Yes," I say, my voice sounding a million miles away, "yeah, I'm fine, just tired. It's been a long five years." I reach for the guitar again and Jed passes it to me. This time I control myself and somehow the guitar ends up resting on my thigh. *Come on Jonny, one note. Just one.* They are looking at me with hope on their faces and lips clamped between teeth. They want me to play. The anticipation hangs in the air, and I don't know what to do. I don't even know if I could play. I don't know the notes… I'm not that version of myself anymore. I'm here to find the music but Jonny Raven stopped existing five years ago. *Bullshit, Jonny Raven is in there, he just needs to be let out.* I sigh and run my thumb down the strings and the sound fills my ears. It's deafening. Strange.

148

Uncomfortable. I turn the pegs and listen again. Just off, only slightly. I turn the peg and strum again. Got it.

"Are you sure you're alright, you are really sweaty." Jed says as I hand him back the guitar.

"It's hot in here."

"It isn't."

"I'm hot. Can you open the window," I ask Ben. He gets up from his seated position on the floor and opens the window. The soft ocean breeze comes in and I catch my breath. My hands shake as I reach for Taylor's guitar but if he notices he has the good grace not to say anything. I tune it and match the tone to Jed's before I do the same with Kyle's. "Ok, you're good to go."

They sling their guitar straps over their shoulders and Ben counts them in. The tuning has helped and the boys' play. I turn from them to face the window, closing my eyes and letting their sound take me outside of the castle, away from the mistakes and the failures to somewhere I remember being. They play the song over and over while I listen, giving them suggestions, letting them put their slant on the music, but underneath it, underneath the rawness of their teenage ambitions, I hear myself. Is it in my head, the hum that rests an octave lower than their young voices, or is it out loud?

"Let's take a break," I say abruptly, stopping them mid-way through. "You must be starving," I glance down at my watch, "Jesus, we've been at it for hours." I lead them down the stairs to the kitchen and take bread, sandwich fillings and fruit from the fridge. In one cupboard are bags of crisps, in another sweet treats. Piling it all onto the table, I hand out plates, knives and fill more glasses with squash.

They chatter happily as they fill their plates, handing items around to each other until they have everything they want. I take an apple from the table, a beer from the fridge, and leave them to it, walking out the cellar door and sitting down at the patio table. I don't know how I feel about all this, and

149

whether having the kids here has been a monumental mistake. It's forcing me to remember how things were when I was their age, burning with ambition and fire and a raw talent. There wasn't a voice like mine in the industry, there still isn't, and what I had right in the beginning, was the absolute conviction that I was going to succeed. It wasn't just about the money, the women, the excesses, it was the belief that I was never going to be a failure like my fucker father. Success may have turned to failure, but I still made it. No one can take that away from me. It's one thing, I suppose. The kids don't have the same convictions in their voices that I recognise from when I started out, but they are hardworking and they have talent, plus they are good looking enough to interest the girls. Maybe they will make it one day.

What about you? Ah, who the fuck knows about me. I have no idea. *Yes, you do.* My fingers flex involuntarily. I held a guitar. I fucking held it. It didn't feel right, it wasn't mine, but the instinctive reach for Jed's instrument, the shape of it on my thigh, the feel of the neck in my hand, the sound of the strings underneath my thumb, that was real. Really, really fucking real. My hands tingle and I'm drawn to tap out a sound on the glass tabletop. This is the second time in as many days that I've felt a vibration, a rhythm, but hoping that it's all coming back seems too risky even if I can't shake the feeling that I hummed. I'm sure I heard it, the husky tone, so unique, that sold millions of records, but I can't ask the lads. They want a rock star, and the reality of my shit would be a disappointment. They need to have the belief that they will make it. I'm not taking that away from them.

I have a long swig of beer.

From here I can hear their laughter and the sounds of chords being played. They have enthusiasm, I'll give them that, so, draining my beer, I give up my solitude and walk back into the kitchen, putting the uneaten apple back into the bowl. "Ready to go again?" I ask.

150

The band have left, their guitars and the saucepans remaining in the lounge. The silence is suddenly more than I can deal with. They had changed songs midway through the practice and played something else I'd written, a newer song called *Changing Lanes*. It was meant to be about becoming a dad but while Susie was at home, heavily pregnant, I was in Santa Monica filming the video and shagging two models from the shoot. I screwed my wife and my daughter over, even then.

I open a bottle of beer and take it out to the terrace, sitting down in the chair nearest the wall, and put my feet up. The ocean is so still that it's hard to envisage the violent storms that Julie mentioned. I wonder what the ocean is doing in Cornwall and if Molly has gone down to the beach yet. I hope she has. I hope her near-death experience doesn't put her off for life.

I drink the beer and watch as the seabirds bob on the water. It must be quite nice to be a bird. No stress, no emotional shit, no failures to be reminded of. I lean back in the seat and close my eyes. I wish it was as easy as bobbing on the water. I wish I knew who the fuck I wanted to be. It's not enough to just want the music back, I need to know who Jonny Raven is. I have no identity, aside from being a failure and a drunk. I know I can't go back to the selfish prick I was because I've learned that lesson but there is safety in the gloom and nothing to sabotage if I wallow in the misery of a life lost.

I wonder what Chelsea is doing. I feel relief to be away from her anger, even though it was me that caused it all. I don't blame her for anything, but it would be easy to rather than shoulder all the responsibility. No, it's all on me, and I can be man enough to accept that. She will be fine and eventually she'll find someone else to give her the life she craves. I just wish that life wasn't going to take what is left of the sweet girl I met. *Sweet and slutty, Jonny, she knew what she was doing.* Yes, she did.

I drain the beer and discard the bottle onto the table. A seagull lands on the wall and eyes me with its beady yellow gaze. "Stop staring at me," I mutter, leaning my head back again and closing my eyes. Of all the women in my life, Chelsea is the only one I've ever been faithful to but that was because I was drunk, broke and holed up in Cornwall waiting to die. There was no way I would have been faithful if I'd still been a superstar. Our marriage would have ended years ago, and I would have moved on to someone else before Chelsea had even packed.

Yet, for Molly I'd be faithful forever. Forever. I can almost feel her arms around me, as they were in Cornwall while she saved me from the darkness. I would never have survived the storm if she'd not been there, but Molly is more than the person who saved me, she gave me hope and in return I gave her...I've no idea. Her flat? That was just cowardly. I should have just gone to her and told her the truth. I should have said the three little words to her because I know that she would be the first and last person I would ever say that too. One day, I'll tell her. Whether it's too late or not, I'll tell her everything.

I wish she was sitting on the terrace with me, understanding in her quiet, gentle way how much hearing my songs being played has affected me. More than I'd like to admit. I wish she was holding my hand while I faced up to the brutal truth. She'd tell me that it was all ok and remind me that I was here to find acceptance and that I have to strip away all the years of self-loathing and the harsh, destructive rhetoric, until I find my way back. The longing for her is breath taking and everything I've tried to bury begins to bubble in my chest. It feels like I'm having a heart attack.

The sound comes, feral and guttural, breaking out of me with such force that it almost blows the seagull off the wall. The roar echoes around the castle, scaring the crows nesting on the roof. I don't stop. I let it come, let the suffocating tightness wrap itself around me and I give in to the feelings, sobbing and writhing with the agony of everything I've been holding inside. I hear Molly's name over and over, as I scream for her, begging and pleading that she'll come for me. That she will wait, that she will love me too and accept me for the fractured man that I am. I will be everything she needs, and I will love her. I will love her forever. Someone hears me, and believes the promises because the tidal wave subsides, and silence comes. I am floating somewhere outside of myself and it's peaceful, so peaceful. I let the silence begin piece me back together, slowing starting to heal the wounds. They are still rotten and raw, but the edges aren't so defined. I can feel the stitches and with it comes the lightness. I am healing. Stitch by stitch. It will take time, but the journey has finally begun.

Molly

Even with the music blaring through the hotel, there is a silence. After days with Aria's bright, bubbly chatter the hotel has been plunged into a stillness that feels unnatural. She was a delight. Funny, self-depreciating and filled with a zest for life that was infectious. Now I'm alone again and staring at the largest bouquet of flowers I've ever seen in my life. Jonny said he was a man of excess, and he wasn't kidding. The delivery man could barely lift them from the van when he brought them five minutes ago. There weren't enough vases to split them into, so I've used buckets from the housekeeping cupboard and the sweet scent has finally covered the festering smell of damp.

I send pictures to Ella.

'Oh my God, Moll, the man is smitten,' she texts in reply. 'Smitten.'

'He was just saying thank you,' I write back.

'Thank you is a thirty quid bouquet from FloraDora, that is a mega buck message. He's got it bad for you.'

'I looked after his daughter!'

'Again, thirty quid would have done, or maybe forty given she didn't end up being sold by some pervert kidnapper! I'm telling you, Moll, this weird fucked up love story is your future.'

'Hmmm.'

'You know it! Right, bugger off, I have work to do! Go and paint a wardrobe or something!'

I look out the front door at the ground floor furniture that Aria and I wrestled out of the hotel before she left yesterday. It's all lined up on the driveway and needs moving before the workmen come tomorrow to strip out carpets, steam off wallpaper and basically turn the whole place into a shell. I'm days behind. Aria was a great distraction from the thoughts that have filled my head, but my timetable of work is completely off. I'm going to have to go at superspeed today. I pour another coffee from the cafetiere on the reception desk and, putting my phone in my pocket, I head out into the sunshine.

The whole task feels overwhelming. Every item from downstairs is outside, and in need of restoration after the storm damage. I love working with furniture and it became a real solace away from Paul's ongoing negative narrative but one at a time seems so much more manageable than everything all at once. I put my phone down on a cabinet and jog back inside to get the portable speaker. Music will help. I link my phone with the speaker and find a radio station. "Right then, Molly. Let's do this." I check each piece slowly, carefully, setting aside what can be worked on, and leaving what is too damaged beside the skips.

I lose the day to the task. Singing along to the radio and studying my vision boards, I work out where each item will go. By the time the sun has turned a soft orange I have rooms laid out on the driveway and furniture paint on order. I'm exhausted. My arms ache and my back feels in a permanent stoop. My phone beeps with a message from Aria. She has written a long text about her journey to Egypt and sends a picture of the view from her hotel. The next message comes quickly with a reminder of the colours she wants in her room in Jonny's suite and a series of emojis. I type out a reply and send a picture of the view in front of me. She's a great kid and I will miss her. I'll miss Susie too. A friendship developed rapidly, and it will be strange that we no longer have a reason to be in touch.

I sit down on a patch of grass with a bottle of wine and some cheese and biscuits to look out over the sea. It's the perfect scene – a low sun sending tawny ripples over the horizon and a calm, flat ocean. Above me are the faint twinkles of the stars and sitting just behind the hotel is the crescent moon, waiting for its time to shine in the heavens.

I feel like I've achieved something this week – maybe it's self-belief, maybe I've proved to myself that I am so much better than Paul ever wanted me to believe. I don't understand how it all went so wrong, and I try to piece it together in my mind, but my thoughts take me elsewhere. They take me to Jonny, alone in his castle, and the pull to him is so physical I could almost run there. I remind myself that I'm super cross with him for forgetting about Aria, but it doesn't stop the ache. I pour another glass of wine. This needs to stop, it's becoming too much of habit, but not tonight. Tonight, the wine can stay, which is just as well because the next song to come on the radio is Jonny's. His throaty vocals seem to wrap themselves around me until there is nothing but him. I squeeze my eyes shut, trying to keep him out, but all I can see is Jonny, looking down at me, his silver wolf eyes full of fire, and I feel the kiss, his arms around me, the perfect moment so vivid. "Goddamn you, Jonny," I whisper, my throat hoarse from keeping the tears at bay, "goddamn you."

The wine doesn't last very long but the plate of food remains untouched as I sit looking out to sea until the final flicker of sunlight fades. Wearily, I drag myself up and back inside, leaving everything on the desk and locking the door. I wander through to the bar and curl up on the sofa, wrapped in a blanket and fall into a dreamless sleep.

***

I wake with a headache and a dry mouth. Urgh, perhaps an excess of red wine isn't the way to solve the Jonny problem. I roll off the sofa and manoeuvre to standing, filling a glass of water from the tap behind the bar. The sofa is the last item to move outside but I'll ask the workmen to lift it. It's solid and heavy, too much for Aria and me to have done. I down the water in one and stretch my aching body. I couldn't feel like this every day, and there is the risk of that if I keep opening bottles. I glance up at the clock. Shit, I have an hour before the crew arrives. Shit, shit, shit. I hurry to the kitchen to make tea and toast, which I take up to my suite. I finish the toast in minimal bites and stand in the shower until the fuzz in my head clears. I'm back downstairs in time to wriggle the furniture from the driveway onto the patchy grass before the team arrive.

Thankfully, they're late. When the vans roll to a stop, I'm midway through sanding down the first side table.

"Molly Bloom," one asks jumping down from the cab.

"That's me," I say lifting my mask and wiping my hands on a cloth. "Hi."

"Hi," he says. "I'm Neil. You ready for us?" He nods at all the furniture.

"Yep, I sure am!" I grin, "I'm glad you're here, I need some help getting all this into the skip."

"No worries!" Six other men get out of the vans and come over to introduce themselves. One I recognise from the bar I was in before the storm, but as there is no recognition reciprocated, I say nothing. They follow me into the hotel, and I give them job sheets, which I leave them to read while I make tea and coffee.

"This is all pretty easy stuff," Neil says taking the tea tray from me. "I was half expecting we'd end up having to rebuild everything."

I shake my head, "thankfully it is mostly just flood-damage, apart from the conservatory which took a real battering."

Neil says, "we will be doing that last, the glass is on order." He pauses, "you're happy with the terms that we agreed?"

"Very. Your quote was great. I have the first payment to transfer to you this morning. Why?"

"The owner's accountant rang me, wanting a full breakdown of what the money would be covering."

"He bloody didn't?" I ask crossly.

"Yeah, but I told him the agreement was with you, so any problems with what I provided was between you and me."

"He's such a dick." I shake my head and smile, "the man has no faith, but I have the cash in my bank account, so he can go whistle. Sorry that he worried you, but I am standing by what we've agreed. Shall I show you around again? I know you've already had the tour, but it will probably be good to see if you spot anything that wasn't picked up on last time."

We carry our mugs as we walk around the building. He takes detailed notes for each room. "I can't see anything that's different to what we discussed. What are you going to do while we strip it all?"

"I'm planning to stay here because I want to refurbish all the furniture that survived the storm. I haven't been able to empty the bedrooms yet, so if anyone can help me, that would be great." Neil nods, "I will probably stay in town when you get to my room. I've not really decided yet, but the dust may drive me out to a clean, dry hotel!"

"I can understand that!" He picks at the wallpaper in the bedroom we're standing in and a chunk of plaster comes off with it. "Oh, shit."

"Don't worry about it. The wallpaper has been up since the dawn of time and will probably bring the building down when you take it off! I'm fearful that every room will end up needing a replaster!"

"Don't worry, love, we'll get this place ready for you!"

I nod. "Excellent." We leave the bedroom and walk down two flights to the ground floor. "The painters have a confirmed date, but I can move them if this work takes longer."

158

"We'll go as fast as we can without compromising on our standards."

"I know and I appreciate that!"

"It was some storm!"

"It really was! I thought it was going to end the world," I grin as we reach reception. "The building shook, windows fell in, the sea reached the stairs, it was unbelievable."

"I bet." He gestures to the buckets of flowers either side of the stairs, "lovely flowers, someone must think a lot of you."

"Apparently so." I say, non-committedly. Neil looks at me strangely but doesn't comment. "If you can lend me a couple of men to get the damaged furniture into the skips, it would be a great help, I can arrange for them to be emptied then."

"Sure thing." He calls out to three of the six and I show them what needs to be skipped. Neil and I walk through the ground floor while he makes more notes on the job sheet and runs his hand down walls, lifting the corners of the carpets to check the floors. I'm relieved that he doesn't look too concerned.

When we reach the kitchen, I say, "please just help yourselves to anything in here. There's plenty to eat and drink, and I have booked another delivery for later in the week so I can top up on anything you want." I lead him down the corridor to the chapel. "The weather is supposed to hit the thirties so if it gets too hot, bring towels and use the pool whenever you want."

"The lads will love this."

"It's a perk of the job. I will move all this -" I wave my arm in the direction of the painted frames and pile of prints on a lounger, "- I just had nowhere to store it all but I think I'm going to need to order a container or something to put everything that I'm working on. Do you have any recommendations?"

159

"My mate will sort you out, I'll ring him. So, what was wrong with all of these?" He asks looking at one of the prints.

"They were so dull, it made me depressed to look at them. I think whoever put them up just stuck them wherever there was a space. We painted the frames, and I've sorted them into the rooms where I think they will look the best. Mind you, I won't really know if I've chosen correctly until the hotel has been decorated. I will need to add to them, but I think the accountant would have a heart attack if I ordered too many new prints!" I laugh, "I may need to scour the charity shops first!"

"He sounds hard work."

"Like you wouldn't believe but arguing with people who pay the bills is part of the job." I regale him with a tale of a client in Hertfordshire who wanted an elaborate décor, and her husband went mad and refused to pay. "He paid in the end," I say. "She wanted pink, he wanted beige and as he was paying, he wanted his way! In the end he gave into her. He must have really loved her because the whole downstairs was pink, the brightest pink you could imagine! She was so happy that she gave me a massive tip!"

"Rich people, hey?!" He says laughing. "We have a lot of that too. I just let them argue and once it's calmed down, I remind them that they owe me money and they have fourteen days to pay, then I get out of there as fast as I can!"

I giggle, "it's the fun of the job."

"So, how did you end up doing this all by yourself?"

I tell him the story and his mouth falls wider and wider as I speak. Even to my ears it sounds unbelievable.

"You're joking?"

I shake my head, "nope. But, as it turns out the storm has done me a huge favour. This sort of job would not have come my way if I'd not been washed up. It's too much for me to do all the painting, so I've got a team coming in, but otherwise, yep, it's all on me!"

"Remind me, who owns this property?"

"A guy called Jonny."

"Jonny?" He looks quizzically at me, but I hold his gaze. "Yes, I remember now, he's famous, isn't he?"

"So I'm told."

"You don't know then?"

"I only what he told me." I don't want to get into any conversations about Jonny. I'm nervous that I'd give something away and end up splashed all over the papers, and also because I feel so protective over Jonny and his wellbeing that talking about him would feel like a betrayal. "It's not really any of my business, I'm just here to do a job." I change the subject and grin, "I just heard a van beeping, that may be my paint."

"Paint?"

"For the furniture. I'm sanding it all down and repainting. It's as dark and dingy as the paintings." I skip off along the corridor towards the front door, thanking the heavens for the van arriving at the perfect moment. Signing for the paint, the delivery driver unloads it onto the drive, and I check it all off against the order. This will give me something to do while the hotel gets stripped but I'm not sure it will be enough to keep my mind silent.

✱✱✱

It's hot work. The sun blazes down and dust sticks to the sweat that is pouring off me as I sand down the furniture. The air feels thick inside the mask and my eyes sting as perspiration seeps into them. The workmen are bright red, and most have taken off their tee shirts, bodies slick with the heat and the grime. They huff and puff as they lift carpets and rugs out to the skip. They work quickly, particularly in this temperature until Neil comes over.

"I was wondering if it would be alright with you if we come in early, say six-ish and leave at two, the lads are struggling with this temperature and it's only going to get hotter." He sits down next to me and runs his hand over the coffee table I'm working on.

"It's fine with me. I'm finding this hard going and I'm not moving!"

"You've done a good job."

"Thanks!" I grin, putting the sander down and moving the mask up to my head. "There are lollies in the freezer, I'll go and get them." I strip the mask off my head and wipe my face on the bottom of my tee-shirt, smearing dust into streaks. "How are you getting on?"

"Everything is out of the downstairs rooms, but we are running out of skip space to add much else."

"I'll get them emptied."

"Thanks."

I stand up and stretch out. "I think I've had enough for today. It's just too hot."

I leave Neil updating the job sheet and head to the kitchen to make lugs of iced squash and find the lollies. Handing them out to the seven men flopped on the grass, I make a quick call to the skip company and join them. Conversation is stilted, it's too hot and they're too tired and even my suggestion of a dip in the pool seems too much. "Why don't you all head off," I say. "Carry on tomorrow morning when it's cooler."

"Are you sure?" Neil says as the men visibly sigh with relief.

"Yes, the skips are being emptied this afternoon as they have space, so it will all be ready for you when you come back. I don't plan on doing anything other than having a cold shower, so yes, please finish today, I would hate for anyone to keel over with heatstroke!"

"Do you want to see what we've done?"

I nod and force my tired body back up. Neil shows me empty room after empty room. The dining room tables were too damaged to be saved so they have gone out to the skip along with the curtains and carpets, the bar still has the sofa in it, and the grand piano from the lounge remains in place. "I've spoken to my mate," Neil says, "he is bringing two big containers up tomorrow, one for this -" he gestures to the piano, "- and one for you. He has them spare, and he owes me a favour so no charge, unless you want to get him some beers?"

"I'll add them to the shopping list. I was worried about the piano because it has sentimental value to the owner."

"Anything else sentimental?"

"I don't think so. I've not been into his suite, but I know it all needs boxing up, so I'll do that before you go in." I should have done it when Aria was here, but I wasn't ready to walk into a space that was completely Jonny. I wasn't ready to smell the scent of him. It's bad enough that I feel him everywhere as it is. Despite overseeing the decorating, I don't have to paint a wall, so leaving it to the crew was perfect. It didn't occur to me that he wouldn't have done it before he left, and I couldn't ask Aria to do it. I wasn't sure what she'd find.

"He didn't do it?"

"I think he left quickly. It was grim here."

The offices are empty of carpets but the storm didn't damage any of the things inside, so I left them as they were. The contents of Jonny's office were put into boxes, a job I gave to Aria. When I have time, I need to go through it all to back up what my reports have found, but that's a job for a rainy day. We exit the hotel and I lie back on the grass, unwrapping my lolly. The sky is so blue it's almost burning my eyeballs, there isn't a cloud to be seen, and in the tired lull the sounds of the sea rolling onto the pebbles drift up the hill. Someone snores and everyone laughs wearily. I roll over and look at my notebook. So much to do, and time is passing quicker than I expected. Using my remaining strength, I stand up and check over the sanding. The paint pots glint in the sunlight and I move them from the drive into reception. "I'm done," I say to Neil, "thanks for today, I'll see you all tomorrow."

He gives me a small wave and I head up to my suite. Standing under a cool shower, I watch as the water turns a dusty brown. So gross. The water is invigorating, and I wash myself free of dirt and sweat then get dressed into the lightest clothes I can find in my pitiful packing. By the time I get back downstairs, the workmen have tidied their tools and have left for the day.

I walk down the driveway towards the sea. Maybe I'll hire a car and get out for a few days in the next couple of weeks, just take a break from all these memories of Jonny and refocus. I could book into a spa, get Ella down and have some girlie time away from all the mess, but I'm held back by the fear that the conversation would just be about Jonny. I know she believes that Jonny has feelings for me, but despite everything that's happened recently, I still can't get past the memory of him letting me go.

I cross the road and walk down the steps to the beach. Am I just here to gain his approval? I wonder if history is just repeating itself but there is no guarantee that mine and Jonny's paths will ever cross again. He may stay in Scotland permanently, he may get his music back and be a superstar again – there is no need for him to see me - I'm not going to be here once the hotel is finished, and besides, my dealings are only with the accountant and the lawyer, not him. Maybe I should just stop hoping and focus on what I'm here for. It's business. That's all. The flowers, my flat and his faith in me are just grand gestures for him to hide behind.

I walk along the beach away from the hotel and cross under the sea bridge to take the cliff path up over the moor. Town isn't far although during the storm it may as well have been on the moon. Despite the heat, it is the place to be today because I need to be out in the world. It may only be a simple reprieve, but I need a coffee in a coffee shop and food I've not prepared myself. I need magazines and books and something else to see other than the dankness of the hotel. I quicken my pace and eventually climb the steps that lead up to the town.

The steps stop at the end of the high street, and I pause for a moment to catch my breath. There is an array of brightly painted shops either side of the flag-stoned path and I walk along, glancing into each shop front as I go until I come to a newsagent. I pop in for a celebrity magazine, also picking up some home-and-garden publications, then continue along the street until I find a coffee shop. It's painted pink with an arrangement of fabric flowers around the door. It's cute. I walk in and the little bell tinkles. The café is busy, but I find a table in the window and sit down. The menu is written on a little blackboard and when the waitress comes over, I order a cappuccino and a toasted sandwich, "and maybe a slice of that carrot cake," I add grinning.

The celebrity magazine holds my attention for a while. It's not particularly interesting, just filled with the antics of reality tv stars. I hate reality tv. The waitress brings over my order and I eat it while flicking through the house magazines, borrowing a pen to scribble notes on pages that inspire me. There is more in the magazines than I imagined. I finish my lunch and order another coffee, munching on the cake whilst looking at the product websites advertised. I add items into baskets, sending an imaginary V to the accountant who will probably be on the phone the moment the receipts are submitted. Fuck him.

I'm never blasé about a client's money, but Jonny trusted me to spend it wisely, and I can justify everything I've spent. Most of what I've bought will be covered by the insurance, technically replacing like for like, but it's actually

165

more 'what I like', than a good match, not that the insurers need to know that. Leaving my coffee, bag and magazine on the table, I whizz along the street to the newsagent for a notebook, scribbling more notes down with yet more coffee. I feel pretty high on caffeine when I pay my bill and wander along the high street to the top end of town. I'm looking for a clothes shop to stock up on summer items. I can't keep sweating in leggings and I'm not raiding Jonny's clothes for anything else. I should return the hoodie to him but I can't. Not yet.

I find a chain store at the top of the street and stock up on tee-shirts and shorts. None are my style, not by a long way, but it's too hot to care about fashion, or lack of, and besides there isn't anyone other than workmen to see me. I follow the high street and turn the corner that leads back to the beach. The tide has come in and the water looks inviting. I walk down the cliff steps and take my shoes off, paddling along in the sea back towards the peninsula.

Jonny

The days have turned into weeks and despite the slowness of my life here, time continued to tick at its normal, speedy pace and I've not even noticed. I've slept for most of it, hours and hours every night, but since being here drifting off in my bedroom above the sea, comes easily. Even my dreams are quiet. I'm grateful for that, seeing Molly in my dreams and waking to an empty bed was more torment than I needed. My demons have stopped shouting their vicious words, or perhaps I'm just not listening anymore. The hideous isolation of living in my hotel suite, drinking myself to death, seems a million miles away to life now. I am healing in the silence. For the first time ever I'm at peace. For someone who thought green juice and yoga was for pussies, I've joined the felines with morning stretches before miles and miles of walks and runs every day which have added a colour to my skin. I no longer look back at myself from the mirror with pasty, grey skin and dead eyes, instead there is a new face that I'm learning to recognise. I feel stronger. Healthier. Focused. Calmer.

The solitude is a warm hug, maternal in its holding of me, keeping me safe. I am safe here. I can breathe. My father isn't going to find me so far away, and I think it's why I sleep so soundly. I was always so scared that he would track me down, even in Cornwall, just to stick the final nail in the coffin. Hopefully he's dead and my mum is free of the promise that the next beating would be her last - *I'm going to fucking kill you, you slut*. I'll never understand why she stayed with him, accepting beating after beating, and even after we escaped, why she went back after ten years of being free. What hold did he have over her for her to give it all up for his fists to smash into her face again. In the quiet moments I think about everyone I shit on but I can now accept that it was my fame that brought them back. In many ways I must be like my dad, with no thought for anyone other than myself and I hate it. Hate that I could be anything like him. I won't go back to that version of me ever again. *That is because you've changed.* Yes, I have, and in these past months, I've changed more than I would have ever imagined.

The sleep and reflection have been good for me. I don't look on my failings in the same way. Maybe it's because I spend so much of my time reading. There are a lot of self-help books in the library, that I think Julie put there when she knew I was coming. Julie and Mark have been a blessing. They look after me with an unintrusive care - I get home from town, or a walk, to find fresh flowers in the kitchen, or homecooked food in the freezer, a top up of beer, and soft drinks for the lads. They come and go, and I rarely see them, but I always know when they've been in.

I don't mind the absence of a tv. There is enough to watch out of the windows, but sometimes I listen to music and when I do, it's often mine that I put on. I can't help it. It proves that I had something special once, and now I can just listen to it and feel a small sense of pride. I was fucking good. Great. There was a reason no one could touch me when I was up high. I hoped it would bring it all back but any music that I want to feel in my soul, is still too far away. Instead of dwelling I'm still working with the lads who come after school to practice, and I look forward to their jovial company. They are fun and the banter has begun to include me because they are not so in awe anymore. They make me laugh with their cheek, and I'm envious of their ambition.

They work hard and they just may make it. If I ever find my way back, I'll make sure their dreams become a reality. They're good kids. They give me a reason to talk about the old times, and it boosts my ego that they hang off every word. I think they're waiting for me to play something, the hints are not so subtle, but I've not touched a guitar since their first visit and when I catch myself reaching for one, something holds me back. A coldness. As though someone is standing in front of me, saying *no, it's not the right time.* I wonder if there will ever be a right time, and as the days pass, I feel that right time drifting away.

I pull on my running shoes and shrug a high vis jacket on over my tee-shirt. I've found a spot at the top of the hill where my mobile gets a signal, it saves me going into town. Now that everyone knows I'm here - thanks lads - it's not always easy to walk into town and be able to just go about my day. No one really speaks to me, but I've noticed more magazines with my face on are making their way into the little newspaper shop. The journalist took the stripper and a crate of whiskey with more humour that I'd expected. The magazine he writes for keeps printing little stories about me, my songs, concerts and lyrics - maybe he wants another stripper, or two - and as a result the music streams are making my bank account look much, much better.

"All the kids know who you are," Jed told me on Friday as he asked me for yet another autograph for someone in his class, "and the mums have started wearing makeup to the shops, in case they bump into you! It's gross. They're all so old..." I laughed at the face he'd pulled and said, "they're all probably younger than me." He nodded and replied, "yeah, maybe, but aren't you supposed to go with the hot blondes, not the old ones who dye their hair." It opened up a whole conversation about all the women they'd pull when they were famous, and I wanted to disprove their theory, but how could I? I'm living proof that all the hot women want musicians. All that rampant fucking seems like another life. It is another life. Not one I'd want again, unless it was with Molly. I'd have to be dragged out of her bed, if I ever got in it. I fucking hope I do, I want to love every single inch of her beautiful, soft body.

I take a deep breath and focus on the hill. It has become both my nemesis and my saviour. I'm too knackered after reaching the top to even think about sex, or the lack of it. I've

169

been tackling this hill for the last month but running up it doesn't get any easier even though I do it almost daily. Most of the time I have to stop halfway and walk, which is fine. I'm usually reading emails or social media anyway because my phone signal randomly comes to life on the way to the top. "Right, hill, you're mine!" The burn hits my calves almost immediately. Ooof, this will be slow going today, my body doesn't want to cooperate. Sluggish from too much sleep and a breakfast of coffee and pastries isn't the best start to exercise but Julie had left them yesterday and they smelled so good I had to eat them.

I slow to a walk when my phone begins to beep. Messages from Tom Masters still moaning about Molly, that I ignore. He can fuck off. She will be looking after the pennies. I am not indulging in his anti-Molly rhetoric just because he's pissed off because she's done a better job than him at finding my missing... money, investments, castle, everything... I'm not sure what I pay him for. The email from Jim Hartell is brighter, Chelsea has agreed to the divorce terms and has signed the papers. Tom is arranging the settlement, but she cannot make another claim on my estate. Good. The next payment of royalties is due and looks to be substantial. I may have been a shit husband, but Chelsea hasn't done anything to deserve more money, particularly from songs I wrote before I met her. I sit on the top of the hill and scroll through Instagram. Maybe I should start posting on my account now that I'm heading back up the charts. It would be an interesting take on rock n roll by being king of the castle! A meditation-practicing, green-juice drinking, hill-climbing king of the castle! "Jonny, you are a complete pussy," I say to myself and smile. It suits me. For now! I lie back and take a drink from the bottle of water. Tomorrow is the barn dance, and I've promised to go, although I would much rather gouge out my own eyeballs with a teaspoon than be on show. Because I will be. There won't be anywhere to hide.

I groan and spread my arms out over the grass. Perhaps I could just stay here.

The peace is disturbed by my phone ringing loudly. I sigh and roll over, to answer it. It's Freddie. I feel a ridiculous sense of happiness.

"Hello Fred," I answer the call.

"Jonny, how the fuck are you?" His voice booms out of the speaker.

"I'm good thanks, really good. I wasn't expecting to hear from you."

"Yeah well, I had to ring, congratulate you, beg forgiveness for being a twat. You know, Jon, lots of reasons to call. I came to Cornwall to see you but the bird doing your decorating said you weren't there. She was alright, you know, Jon, pretty fucking foxy for a decorator in her tight little shorts..."

"Not your type though, hey?" I try and keep my voice light, but I want to punch him in the face for looking at Molly. I'm not longer feeling the ridiculous sense of happiness.

"These days anything would be my type!" He pauses then says, "so I want to apologise Jon, for the last time we spoke. You have to understand the pressure I was under, and I know, it was fucking tough for you, and it wouldn't have made you feel good that I was almost forced to drop you from our client list. I didn't want to. You know that don't you?"

"Do I?" I sit up and look out at the view.

"Come on Jon, you know it was hard for me, but I've had a lot of time to think and that's why I came to Cornwall to see you..."

"Are you still there?" I interrupt sharply, "in Cornwall?"

"Yeah, I'm at some hotel in the town. The foxy decorator said your place wasn't open. I wish she'd been open..."

Has he always been this disgusting? I suppose he has because he had no reason to be anything else. He always got

171

whatever woman he wanted. It was a perk to being the manager of Jonny Raven, he got my cast-offs. He didn't care, just wanted them to stroke his ego and every other part of his overweight, sweaty anatomy. I shudder but say nothing about Molly.

"So, you came to see me? Why?"

"I made a mistake, mate. I buckled to pressure. I want you to be represented by me again, I want us to be the mates we were until, you know..."

"Until you dropped me? Look, Fred, you're wasting your time, I'm not making any music so there is no point."

"Someone needs to look after your best interests." he says in such a way that he sounds smarmy.

"I'm doing alright on that," I say, "I'm in good shape, I'm not drinking, well, not whiskey anyway. It's all good."

"Is it? So good you're who knows where. Where the fuck are you anyway? The bird at the hotel didn't seem to know."

I don't want to tell him. Every instinct I have is yelling at me to not tell him. "I'm on holiday. Nowhere special. Look, I'm glad you called but really Fred, I don't need representation, there is nothing to represent."

"Tell me where you are and I'll get the new terms sent to you, they're great terms, you'll be pleased." Same old Freddie, not listening to a word I say.

"Why? I don't have a career, Freddie, good terms or not, you're wasting your time."

"I don't think so, and it's a risk I'm prepared to make. The partners agree with me."

I don't understand why he is pushing me so hard. He was so clinical when he dumped me, with no consideration to our twenty-five year friendship. "Hang on, Fred, Aria is calling me. Can you hold?" I press hold and answer the phone to my daughter. "Hi kiddo, how are you?"

"Oh my God, Dad, you're number one. Number One." Her words come out in such a rush that they tumble over each other.

I feel the strangest swooshing sound in my ears. "Huh?" I say, "I'm what?"

"Number One, Dad, I've just heard it on the radio. I'm so proud!"

"What song?" My mouth is so dry that my tongue clicks against my teeth.

"*Brave.*" She says brightly. "I told you everyone was listening to your music after that shitty article. Literally the whole school have posters of you on their walls, which is embarrassing, I mean, you are handsome Dad, but old..."

"Thanks," I'm not sure I'm following the conversation. Number One? It's impossible. *Brave* was released fifteen years ago. It got to number one back then and stayed there for twelve weeks. It's a good song.

"I didn't mean it like that, Dad, it's just, you're my dad and I don't want anyone thinking of you like that, it's weird." She giggles, "I'm so proud of you, Dad, this is awesome. Oh God, idiot Chelsea will be after you for more money."

"She's not getting any more money," I say distantly. It all makes sense now. Freddie must have been watching the charts and timed his visit when Number One was looking likely. "Can you hold on? I just need to do something."

"Yep, but be quick, I've got drama club in a minute."

I switch calls over. "Fred?"

"Hi mate, Aria ok?"

"Yes, she's fine. Tell me, why have you gone to all this trouble to re-sign me?"

"I told you, Jon, I felt bad."

"That's the only reason, is it?" I open a browser on my phone and type in the chart website. There I am, Number One with other songs at Number Ten, Number Eighteen and Number Thirty-Two. Holy fuck. I knew I was being

173

streamed but... tears begin to roll down my face and I'm swamped by feelings of gratitude. That fucking journalist has single-handedly given me my career back. If it hadn't been for his shitty article...I am vaguely aware of Freddie talking out of my phone, and I look down at the charts, trying to believe it as big blobs of tears distort the screen. "Fred," I say eventually, wiping my eyes. "You left me to rot. You can shove your terms up your fat arse." I cancel the call and speak to Aria. "Hey kid, you're right. I am. Number fucking One…"

"Dad!" She says outraged, "language!"

I can't speak. I am swamped by a wave of emotion so great that I can almost understand how Molly felt when the sea came for her. Almost. But not quite. This isn't a life and death situation this is a *holy fuck* situation. I wish Molly was here. I wish she could be next to me as the insane rollercoaster begins again. I just want her by my side. Is Number One enough to ask her for forgiveness, is it enough to ask her to be with me forever. Would she jump with me.

"Dad? Are you crying?"

I can't get my words out. She says nothing, seeming to understand that I can't speak, so she just waits at the end of the phone as tears roll down my face, soaking the front of my tee-shirt. Number fucking One. When everything was lost, and the world fell down around me I never, ever believed that this would be possible, that I would be back at the top.

"Dad? Are you alright?"

"Yes," I say thickly, "yes, I am better than alright."

"Dad, it's amazing."

"It really is."

"Will you be coming back soon?"

"Eventually."

"Can I come for the first part of the summer holidays? I've never been to Scotland!"

"You can come for as long as you like."

174

"Dad, do you think Molly would come?" She asks cheekily, "I think she'd probably like to."

"Do you?" I ask, wiping my eyes, "and why do you think that?"

"Because she totally has the hots for you, she went red every time I said your name."

"You like Molly?"

"I choose her, Dad. I told you I got to choose the next one, and Molly is my choice."

I want to say that she's mine too, because she's the one. Instead, I say, "I'm glad you were the one to tell me all this, Aria. Wow, Number One."

"You'll be great again, Dad, the world will know what I do, that you're the best. I've got to go now, I need to get ready for drama. Well done Dad, you're so cool. Love you," and with that she's gone, and I'm left staring at the bright blue of the ocean sending a silent thank you to whoever is listening.

***

"Jonny?" The voices yell from the kitchen, as the back door slams.

"Up here," I call back. The five lads stomp up the stairs, their trainers squeaking on the polished steps.

"Yo, Jon, Number One," Taylor says grinning, flopping down in the chair opposite me. "Fucking awesome, man!"

I shake my head at the attitude, smiling. "It is fucking awesome!"

"Yeah, congrats, man." Jed says, shrugging his jumper off. "Maybe we should cover that one too, I was listening to it on the way over, it's a great song."

"I think you should focus on your own songs. You've only got space to do three in your time allocation, don't just do my stuff, you need to be looking at your songs, be original. You're not going to get the girls if you're not showing them all the goods!" I grin as Taylor does a couple of hip thrusts. "Calm down, Tay, you're fifteen..."

"I bet you did it when you were fifteen."

"I'm not telling you anything about what I got up to at fifteen, but as a father of a teenage daughter, I'm saying, calm down. Plenty of time to sew your oats, but the local barn dance in a small town is not the place!"

"I'm following your daughter on Instagram!" Kyle says, looking at me from under his fringe. "She's fit, looks nothing like you, does she."

"You can bloody well unfollow her," I say sharply.

Kyle laughs, "chill, I'm not being a stalker, I'm just following her. It's mostly hockey and drama but she did post about you being Number One and that post got thousands of likes. You should be on Instagram and TikTok, get more people buying your music then we'll get famous because of you!"

"It sounds like you've got it all planned. What's TikTok anyway?"

"It's a video site, you can post videos and people like them. It's the way to get seen these days."

"It was so much easier back in the day," I mutter, "we just went on tour, none of this virtual shit."

"Alright, Grandad, calm down!" Kyle grins, "you need to move out of the stone age! In fact, you need to get Wi-Fi here, it's weird that you don't!"

"I don't want it. If I had Wi-Fi I'd never go anywhere."

"Your daughter has TikTok. I follow her on there too!" He says cheekily. I playfully swat him and resolve to have Aria take herself off social media.

"Let's get this painful hour over with, shall we, you kids are driving me to want to drink!" I grumble.

"Are you coming on Saturday?" Billy asks.

"It depends on how badly you murder my songs this week," I say nonchalantly, "are you playing or just talking, because I haven't got all day!"

"What else would you do if we weren't here? Yoga?"

"Maybe. All the rock and rollers are doing yoga know, don't you know!"

"That hippy shit isn't for us!" Billy smirks, and I shake my head slowly.

"Ah, just play, will you! Before I regret having you here."

"You say that every time, Jonny," Jed says putting his guitar strap. "You'd be bored without us."

"Oh, would I?"

"You know it." He strikes a chord and grins.

They form a semi-circle around Ben 's drum kit and he counts them down. The drums are probably too loud for a small, panelled room, but banging saucepans didn't give him the practice he needed. The drums came in a few weeks ago and it's changed the band's dynamic. He's good, probably the best out of the five and has an energy that I recognise. He wants it more than the others, I can hear it when he plays. The more I spend with these kids, the more I feel they will have a great future. They have the cocky self-assuredness of youth and it's an attitude I remember well. They run though their set list and stop.

"What do you think," Taylor asks. "Do we sound good."

"Yeah," I cock my head, "but something is missing. Play it again."

They count in and start playing. I listen closely, feeling a vibration under my fingers. It's an itch that needs scratching, but I can't reach it. It's as though I can feel the song, and I know instinctively what it needs but I can't find the words to direct them. "Play again," I say as soon as they finish. I close my eyes and listen, waiting to hear the whispers, but all I hear is the chanting crowd calling for me *Jonny, Jonny, Jonny* and then I understand. The song needs me. It needs the unique

177

sound that I brought to it, my soul in the words. *I can't,* I whisper back, *I can't do it.* The truth is, I'm scared. Terrified. The fear of trying and failing is too great. *You're scared to fail in front of the lads.* I am. They're great kids and their opinion matters. I don't know why. It just does.

I make them play again and again, listening, guiding, observing and pushing them to dig deeper. By the time we finish the light outside has faded and the bright moon sits above the water. "I think you're done," I say. "I don't think we can get anymore from these songs, this is the best you can be, and it's plenty good enough. The girls will love you!" They grin and puff out their chests. "I'm really proud of you. You're going to do great on Saturday."

"Are you coming, Jonny?" Kyle asks.

"I wouldn't miss it." In truth I'd rather stick pins in my eyes, but I can't let them down.

"You'd better get back on social media," Taylor says grinning, "and video us for TikTok!"

"I'm not going on TikTok!"

"Is Aria coming?"

"Not when you're having inappropriate thoughts, she's not!" I say hotly.

"Is she coming for the summer holidays?"

"Maybe, but I will be locking her away! She's not going anywhere near you horny lot!" I laugh, "now go home, I need to do stuff, and your parents will be missing you."

"What stuff?" Jed asks, "you've got nothing here to do!"

"I have plenty to do, and I need to do it while you're not here. So, off you go. Give your mums my love!"

"Eeeugh, gross!" Kyle says.

"Now you know how I feel when you're being letchy about my daughter. Show yourselves out."

"See you tomorrow?" Taylor asks, suddenly looking pale. "Maybe another run through."

"One more," I say, "you don't want overkill!"

178

"Ok." He says, looking relieved.

"You've got this, lads, they're going to love you. You've worked bloody hard, and it's paid off. Now, please, go home before your mums coming looking for you."

"See you tomorrow," they say one, by one, putting their instruments down and walking out of the room. I can hear them bantering with each other all the way down the stairs before the back door slams and silence falls over the castle. I flop down in the chair beside the window and look out over the sea. Number One. Number fucking One. Today feels like a dream I'm going to wake up from because none of it feels real. For the first time since I've lived here, I wish I had Wi-Fi, just so I could check the charts again. I walk down to the kitchen and take a beer from the fridge, popping the lid off and taking it outside. It's a cool night and a colder breeze is coming off the sea, but I pull a hoodie on and sit in on the terrace, looking at the stillness and despite wanting to celebrate being Number One, all I can think about is Molly.

Molly

"Cheers!" Ella says, raising her glass to me. "I'm so glad you've come home."

"Me too, even if it's just for a few days!" I say, lifting my cocktail in a toast, "it's so nice to be back. I've forgotten what my little flat looked like. It's good to be away from all the dust but I'm missing the sea! The traffic outside my window is keeping me awake!"

"You're not staying in Cornwall, you know that don't you?"

"I know..." I feel a pang when I say it. Bath has always been my home, but I've been like a fish out of water since I've been back. My flat feels claustrophobic, and the unending noise from the cars and lorries wake me up over and over throughout the night. I miss the sea and the space and the sunrise over the water. I miss the fresh, salty air and being able to walk along the shore every day. It's going to be really difficult to leave it all behind, but now that the decorators are in, the time is beginning to tick a lot faster.

"Do you think you will be finished when you said?"

"More-or-less. I've painted the furniture, the new stuff is on order for delivery at the end of the month, I've done all the pictures and the curtains are stored in the chapel. All the bedding, towels and other things are being delivered once the furniture has been installed, so yep, mostly."

"I don't know how you did it all by yourself."

"I have people doing it for me."

"But you had to tell them what to do! Your portfolio is going to be amazing at the end. I'm dead proud of you."

"Thanks! I'm pretty proud of me too!"

Ella takes a sip from her drink and pulls a face, "yuck, I wish I'd not got this two of these now."

"Ah, get it down you! You can choose something else next. That's the perk of Friday daytime drinking with two-for-one cocktails! Even the bad ones are cheap enough to stomach for one round! What cool chicks we are, getting hammered on a workday!" I giggle and lean back in my chair. The cocktail bar is in a prime spot at the top of town, usually perfect for people watching but today I'm not interested in anyone else's life. A car idles in traffic, blasting Jonny's song from the wound down windows. Ella hesitates, looking at me with concern but she doesn't mention the song when she finally speaks.

"You would be cool if you ever got out of that bloody hoodie." She stares at me and sighs, "what are you going to do, Moll?"

"Head back to Cornwall on Monday and keep an eye on things! You wouldn't recognise it."

"That's not what I mean."

"I know, but it's all I can say." I tell her, swilling the cocktail around the glass. "It's been months, Els, and nothing. Not a word."

"Flowers, your flat, his daughter..."

"All lovely, but it's not him, is it? It's not him turning up on the doorstep saying he made a mistake and I'm The One. I mean, what does that even mean, why are we so hung up on finding The One. We've been brainwashed..."

"No, we haven't, we look for our mate because it's basic biology. The One is the person that our body matches with because it's a physical, evolutionary thing. We don't choose, it is chosen for us. It's why we have to kiss the frogs before we find the prince and when we do, we just know and then we mate for life! What if he's your lifer, Moll? Wolves find theirs, penguins, even seahorses have lifelong mates, why would we be any different?"

"Because we're not animals, we're people and he's a rock star, so a different breed entirely! He's probably moved on to someone else...look, I can't talk about Jonny because thinking about him makes me feel sad. I've been on such a high with

181

the renovations, that I don't want to feel low. I just have to accept that he doesn't want me. It's hard because his music is everywhere! His manager even turned up on the doorstep, urgh what a slimeball! Then, he got to Number One yesterday, and I felt so happy for him and so delighted that I messaged Aria. She was buzzing. She's so sweet..."

"It isn't Aria that you should be messaging, Molly. It's Jonny. You should go to him. You are literally the only person in the world who knows where he is. He is all alone. Brooding. Probably thinking about the little lost seahorse who washed up on his doorstep. I still think he's The One for you and this hiccup is part of love's grand plan." Ella knocks her cocktail back and pulls a face, "I'm not sure I can drink the other one."

"Of course you can! Just hold your nose, then you won't taste it." I pick up my glass and swill it before knocking it back in one. Ella looks at me with a frown, as I pick up the second glass and drink it down. "If you can't beat them, join them!" I say and wave at the waiter who comes over. "Four raspberry mojitos please." I silence Ella with a glance. "We are doing the list, and I'm not going home until I'm drunk."

"Ooh good plan!" She giggles, "happy, drunk you is the best!"

"Not sure how happy I'll be," I groan, "I feel all over the place."

"Ah, get over yourself, Moll, you're in your prime! Bin that skanky hoodie and either go to him or find someone else. Take ownership of your own life, you've got rid of Paul the Prick, so either Jonny is The One and you'll go to him and he'll whisk you up into his arms to snog your face off, or he's not and you'll have a cheeky night with a random man later and I'll live the single life by proxy!"

"You wouldn't swap Robbie."

"Not for all the chocolate in the world but it doesn't mean that I don't sometimes long for one night back in my single days!" She puts her feet up on the chair opposite and pushes her sunglasses onto her head. "Do you remember, Moll, being teenagers and going on the pull after raiding your parents' drinks cabinet. We thought we were so cool."

"We've always been cool!" I thank the waiter who places four glasses in front of us. "Plus, going on the pull was safe for me. No chance of falling for anyone who I met on a night out, no swapping numbers, just a snog on the dancefloor at Cadillacs. I had the right idea, much easier to not fall for anyone."

"Jonny isn't dead though, Moll and you need to stop this nonsense and go to him."

"I'm not drunk enough."

"Then drink, woman, drink."

***

I wake up as the train pulls into Glasgow some time around midnight. My head is pounding from the insane number of cocktails that Ella and I drank before we somehow got to London. I don't remember the journey, and I don't remember saying goodbye to her, but I have a carrier bag with new clothes in and a toothbrush that I have no recollection of buying. I'm on the last train, there isn't one back to London until the morning. Fuck. My mouth is so dry that I stop at a coffee wagon and buy some water before asking directions to the nearest cheap hotel. My heart is pounding. I am feeling confused and sick. Really, really sick.

I feel hesitant as I leave the station. There is so much noise coming from bars and people are staggering around, as drunk as I must have been just a few hours earlier. I try and walk by them without drawing attention to myself, keeping my head down and cross the street to the bright orange FirstHotel on the corner beside the station, as the guard said it would be. I ring the buzzer and wait for a tired-looking porter to let me in. There is one room available, so I hand over my credit card and collect the key, struggling to get through the security door into the accommodation. How the fuck did I get here?

I punch Ella's number into my phone as I wrestle with the key card. My head hurts. "Ella?"

"Are you there?" She asks thickly.

"If by here you mean Glasgow, then yes I am. How did I get here?" I rub my dry eyes and drop the bag on the floor.

"No fucking idea. Oh my God, I think I've died."

"I think I have too and ended up in hell. I feel so sick. I've got a bag a of new stuff and no return ticket. What the fuck, Ella." I shiver and my limbs begin to shake as the effects of the alcohol begin to wear off.

"When did you sober up?"

"Dunno, I don't think I have. I passed out." I slump down on the bed. "How much did we drink?"

"Too much," she groans, and I hear retching. "Sorry, Molly, I've been really fucking sick since I got back to Bath. I don't even know why I went to London! Do you?"

"Dunno." I open the water and drink half of it in one go. "Why am I in Glasgow? In what strange fucked up universe was that ever a good idea?"

"I seem to remember that you are there to declare undying love to Jonny, which probably means I went to London with you to either make sure you actually went or because I'm fucking nuts." She retches again. "How come you're not being sick?"

"Because I'm in the twilight zone where the penance is to just feel bloody awful. This room smells of pee." I swallow nausea, "jeez, Ella, it stinks like a men's toilet, I swear it is actually going to make me sick, urgh, hang on..." I rush to the bathroom. It's been cleaned with such strong, cheap bleach that my eyes water. I lift the lid of the toilet just in time.

184

"Moll?" I can hear Ella yelling from my phone. I throw up a few more times, before blowing my nose and flushing it all away.

"I've been sick," I groan at her. "I feel terrible. I shouldn't even be here."

"Maybe it's fate stepping in. I'm glad you're safe Molly, but I have to go to sleep. Double lock the door and ring me in the morning."

"'K. Night." I hang up and lie out on the bed, waiting for the room to stop spinning, before the alcohol sends me into a fast, dreamless sleep. I wake a few hours later feeling as though I've eaten floor scrapings. The bright light comes in through the window and burns my eyes. I groan and roll over, waiting for the nausea to subside before I struggle into the bathroom. I feel gross. Grimy and sweaty and just gross. I strip off my clothes and stand under the shower for the longest time, before making a bitter coffee from the small tray on the desk. I nibble on a sweet biscuit as I look at train times, wanting an escape from Glasgow as quickly as possible. Then I stop. Maybe I should just know. One way or the other. Maybe Ella is right, and I should go to him. I never have to see him again if he turns me down. I change the search and book a train ticket up to the station nearest the castle. "What are you doing, you crazy woman," I say, punching my card number into the booking site. "Go home! Forget this nonsense and go home." I clearly don't listen to myself because in the next breath I'm booking into a B&B in the town close to Jonny. I ring Ella, "oh my God, Ella, I've done it."

"Done what?" She asks sleepily.

"I'm going to Jonny."

"No fucking way!" She yelps, "that's so exciting. I know this will work out for the best, Moll, I just know it. God, you're so brave. Maybe I should have come with you to see

185

the outcome. Fuck it, I'm coming up. Where are you staying?"

I tell her the details. "You can't come all this way though, Els, you've already paid for a return to London."

"You paid for that!" She laughs, "nothing is showing on my card."

"Did I? You're such a cheap date!"

"I sure am! Now bugger off, I need one more vomit before I catch the train!"

Ella hangs up and I unwrap the second biscuit. This is not how I expected my weekend to turn out. Biscuit finished, I get dressed into the clothes I bought and head out into the street. It's already busy. I get bumped by a man who grumpily tells me to 'get out of the bloody way' and have to dodge a family with miserable looking kids as I try to cross the flow of people. I wander into a clothes shop and buy extra clothes because I'm not going to last long in the random joggers and tee-shirt that I bought somewhere by Paddington. I stand in the queue, almost hearing my credit card sobbing in my bag and telling me that this could be the most expensive mistake of my life, but I hand the card over anyway and leave the shop in search of breakfast.

I don't eat much. The divebombing butterflies that have taken up residence in my stomach make me want to throw up its contents, but I eat what I can, pay the bill and re-join the throng until I reach my hotel. The stench of pee has worsened as the temperature has gone up, and I retch a couple of times before I hurriedly pack up my minimal items and check out. Heading to the station I try and talk myself out of going but my legs still carry me onto the platform and into the train. It's a small, single-coach train but I find a seat near the window and stare into nothing as it slowly pulls away. I try to close my eyes but my head hurts, so I just watch the scenery pass as it chugs up the track, taking me far away from hustle of the city. I should have gone back to Bath and stopped this nonsense but the closer I get to Jonny, the braver I feel, and the ferocious butterflies turn into little popping bubbles.

I feel the pull. The nearer I get to him, the more I feel it, tugging at my centre like a magnet until I'm buzzing. This trip was meant to be. Everything that has happened has pushed me to this moment and even if I get it completely wrong, and it's the last time I see him, it will be enough because I will know. I realise that what I need is to be able to piece all the events together and for it to make sense. All of it. Nearly drowning, meeting Jonny, the three days that have been etched into my memory as the most important moments of my life, his extravagant gift of my flat, the huge job to renovate the hotel, Aria - all of it. The outcome isn't clear, and I am walking into the unknown but it's ok, it will take me to the resolution. I'll run if I have to. Either way, I have to see him. Whatever it means for the rest of my life.

The train slows and comes to a stop at a small station. I wait for the five other passengers to disembark before I follow, walking to the exit where a single taxi is waiting. I give the B&B name and climb into the back. He chats away in his musical Scottish accent, pointing out landmarks as we drive along. Once we leave the suburbs there is nothing but blue ocean and green hills, small towns nestled into the backdrop and the occasional puffy cloud. If I wasn't feeling so awful, I would be taking endless photos, but the mere concentration of one snap is enough to make me nauseous.

"Can you show me the castle when we get there, please?" I ask suddenly. "The one on the island."

"Yes, keen on castles, are you? It's owned by a rock star, don't you know?"

"Is it?" I'm not sure I sound as nonchalant as I want to because his eyes flick up to watch me in the rear-view mirror. I give him a small smile and resume looking out of the window at the unending green until the castle looms in the distance. It's stunning. A gasp escapes me, and the taxi driver turns his head towards me.

"Lovely isn't it? It's been there for seven hundred years, not like it is now, it has been rebuilt a few times, but there has been a castle on there for as long as people lived here."

"It's nothing like I imagined," I say quietly. "I thought it would be grey and a bit dull, not glowing and yellow. It's gorgeous."

"Aye," he says, "that it is."

He continues past the castle, and I wonder if Jonny is inside and what he may be doing. Is he thinking of me, or have I been forgotten along with all the other women, especially now that he's topping the charts again. My head thuds as the hangover reminds me that it's in control and I sip the water bottle from my bag. The taxi slows as it comes into the town and stops outside of a small, thatched B&B, a little wooden sign swinging in the breeze. I pay the driver and he helps me with my carrier bags, taking them up to the door. I knock and a short blonde-haired woman opens, her smile beaming from her soft, rosy face. I was expecting someone running a B&B to be older but she looks the same age as my mum.

"Welcome, welcome," she ushers me in, carrying my bags for me despite my protestations. The cottage is cool and has a light smell of roses, it reminds me of my Gran's garden, and I relax. Nothing bad ever happens when there is the smell of roses. She introduces herself to me as Mary and shows me to a twin room at the top of the cottage under the eaves.

I want to ask about the solitary man in the castle, but I am suddenly scared of what she would think of me if I did. Instead, I compliment the room and she kindly offers to make me a cup of tea. I unpack my meagre items and put my toiletries into the little ensuite shower room. Mary comes back in with a pot of tea and some shortbread. She sits down on the chair in front of the mirror and chatters away, little facts about the area and places to see. I half listen, feeling bad that she is so enthusiastic and all I want to do is run back down the coast to Jonny. He's here. We are in the same place. I don't care about the local barn dance and how the whole town turns out for a night of festivities.

"My grandson is playing in a band tonight. He has been up at the castle with the others most days practicing, and they've gotten really good. He wants to be a rock star. I used to think he was dreaming but I heard them the other day as I was walking along the coastal path, and they were much better than I'd expected.

"They play at the castle?"

"Yes, the musician who lives there has taken them under his wing, I suppose he knows what it's all about. He's going tonight, it's the talk of the town." She smiles lightly, "the hairdressers can't cope with the demand from all the ladies, he's quite the catch apparently!"

"Is he," I ask dully.

"So I'm told, too young for me, I'd rather Jon Bon Jovi!" She laughs and I giggle. "You should come if you've got no plans, it's always a great night, lots of sore heads the next day."

"I've got a sore head already, but yes, I'd like to come, thanks."

"What brings you all the way up here?" She asks, plumping the pillows.

I don't know what to say. I can't lie to her, but also, I can't really say *the hot rock star in the castle.* She waits and eventually I say, "peace."

"I can understand that, life down south always seems to be so manic. You'll enjoy the quiet up here. I'll leave you to settle in. There is a key beside the front door, so if you want to have a walk around town, then just take it."

"Thank you."

189

She hovers in the doorway. "The barn dance is at seven. I'll be walking up then."

"Thanks. My friend will be arriving quite late, is it ok for her to stay here too, as I've got a twin room?"

"Yes, I often have late arrivals, but maybe she could give you the time she's likely to be here, then I know to be back."

"She can come and find us at the barn dance, I'll let her know." I smile and pick up the cup of tea. "I think I may have a nap after this. I suddenly feel worn out."

"Sore heads will do that to you!"

Mary closes the door behind me, and I open the little window letting the breeze in. Jonny is helping the band with their music? This feels monumental. I wonder if he's singing or writing, or whatever it is that he needs to do. I hope so. I hope he's got it all back and is ready to take on the world again. I don't want to think that he is still broken and grieving for the part of his life that meant so much to him. I think about Jonny as my eyelids close and restful sleep comes. When I wake I feel much better and with time to spare, I head out into the afternoon.

The high street is quaint and old fashioned but with a really happy vibe. Nothing is open but as its nearing dinner time I walk into the pub and order food. I'm hungrier 'than I thought and clear my plate, washing it down with lemonade. Every time Jonny's name is mentioned my ears prick up. It seems that he has become an enigma, living out on his island, rarely coming to town, and something about that makes me feel better. Maybe there is hope, after all.

Jonny

The lads are as white as ghosts as they look out from behind the curtains at the crowd filling the barn.

"I don't want to do this," Taylor says, his words clipped, "they're going to laugh at us, then we'll never pull anyone."

"It's good to be nervous," I say handing him a glass of water, "makes your senses work harder, you'll hear each other better and feel the music more. Do you think it's easy to stand on a stage in front of one hundred thousand people? Nope, it's the same as if you were standing on a small stage in the middle of nowhere in front of people you know. Take some deep breaths. You've been practicing every day for weeks! You've got this. You'll smash it out of the park, and all those girls you go to school with will want your phone numbers by Monday."

"Aria may want it too!" Kyle grins, "she's following me back."

I shake my head slowly, "I will say this just once more, stay the fuck away from Aria with your raging teenage hormones!"

They all laugh and check their instruments, Ben ensuring that his drum kit is locked together properly. They have worked hard, they are great kids and I want them to shine. I remember what it's like to be out on stage for the very first time, with fire and passion and overwhelming ambition. I want them to love every moment of this experience, to be the best they can be, and I have an almost paternal pride in them. My hands tingle and there is a vibration under my skin. It's a vibration that has been growing over the weeks, and I can almost hear something that I've not heard since my last concert. Whispers. Flickers. It's not the demons, they have stopped calling to me, it's something else. I think it may be hope.

"Are you ready lads?" The farmer comes up, "you're on."

191

"I'm gonna be sick," Billy says turning green.

"If you need to be sick, go and do it now." I tell him and one by one they leave the backstage for the field behind.

"Who'd want to be famous hey?" The farmer laughs, his bright red face turning redder.

"No idea." I say, grinning. The lads come back, swilling water around their mouths. "If you're quite finished being pussies…"

"Says the man who does yoga!"

"… your crowd awaits."

The farmer heads out on stage and gives a roaring introduction, then the curtains part, the spotlights go on and the lads start.

The crowd goes fucking nuts. It's filled with parents and kids, teenagers who are trying to look cool but end up singing along. My song sounds new, edgy and fun and they absolutely nail it. I keep back, out of the way, hidden by the makeshift curtain. It's their spotlight, not mine and I wonder if my destiny lies along a different path now, as a manager or songwriter, not as a singer, no longer the rock star I was. *No, Jonny, your path is winding back, the detour is over.* I feel my hands tremble, the vibrations pulsing along my fingers until I can see the light particles dancing in front of me. Somehow, I miss the end of the set, miss hearing the crowd cheering and asking for more, and the red, sweaty faces of the lads going back out, to do one more song. My song. My Number One. They kill it and then they're speaking and it's my name I hear, *Jonny, Jonny, Jonny* and Jed is taking me by the arm and leading me out but now I don't want to run, and hide and live a life waiting to die. I want to live. The stage is tiny, but I'm on it, with lights shining in my face and above all the chants I hear one voice. It's the voice I've been so desperate to hear, and I wonder if I'm now worthy, if I've learned enough, if she will forgive me and if she does then I will promise to never let her go.

192

There is an electric guitar in my hand and the strap ends up over my shoulder. The crowd are calling my name, their voices roaring as one and with their chants Jonny Raven is back. The tiny crowd, this tiny stage inside a barn has brought me back to myself. I can feel the energy and the anticipation. They are waiting for me until suddenly, there is only silence. One collective intake of breath and they wait. I look down at the guitar then out at the crowd. The sea of faces merge into one and all I see is her. Gazing up at me, her blue eyes wide and elfin hair sticking out from where hands have raked through it.

"Molly?" I whisper, closing my eyes and giving my head a shake. It can't be. I look again and in front of me, with her lip clamped between her teeth, tears rolling down her face, is Molly.

She's here.

She's fucking here.

My heart swells in my chest and I can't breathe. Have I done enough? Have I repaid the universe for all my sins? If Molly is here then there can't be any more debt for them to claim. It was all worth it - every single battle with the devil was worth it - because she came.

Molly nods slowly, urging me on, a gentle smile of hope on her beautiful face. *Do it,* I can hear her say, *come on Jonny, do it.*

I strike a chord. The crowd burst out with a cheer and Molly's gentle smile becomes a beaming grin, brighter than any light above me. I strike another chord, then another and the recognition begins to flood her face.

Her mouth forms words *Oh my God* and she knows the song, knows it's for her.

I step closer to the microphone, not taking my eyes off her and speak to the crowd. "This isn't a song I would have ever planned to do," I say, my fingers moving on the strings instinctively, "and I'm not sure I know all the words, so if you

193

know it, help me out!" I laugh, "the rock star in me is mortified, but-" I play a reef, "-this song is dedicated to the most amazing woman that I have ever met. Molly, this is for you."

She's wiping her eyes and I wipe mine with one hand, the other still strumming the guitar. The melody comes naturally, and I play it without thinking, but the words get lost. I don't know them well enough but the crowd sing along and I muddle through. Who would have ever thought I'd be playing some boy-band shit on my way back from hell. But, I do. Because it's for her. The little waif who swept up to my door, is singing along with me and she knows. She knows what she's done, and that I wouldn't be here without her. It is all for her. My love.

I don't finish playing. I shrug the guitar off my shoulder and lay it on the stage before jumping down. Those at the front of the crowd move aside and in the next moment, she's in my arms, her soft mouth under mine and I'm kissing her like my life depends on it. Because, it does. She is my life. She is my everything. She is the reason that the sun shines.

"You're here." I murmur against her lips, and she kisses me with such intensity that everything stirs. "Don't fucking kiss me like that, it's not decent!"

Molly laughs and drops little kisses along my jaw. "I can feel how indecent it is."

"Well, stop it then! This is a family show!"

"I'll never stop." She says, holding my face in her warm palms. "I'll never stop kissing you, Jonny."

I plant a kiss on her mouth. "Good..."

"You did it," she whispers and I'm aware of music coming from the stage. The lads are back out, Ben is counting them down and Billy speaks to the crowd.

"As our mentor is currently busy, we thought you may like another from us. This is one we wrote." The band launch into their song and I pull Molly to me.

194

"You really did it, you're back!" She says, her voice breaking.

"I did it because of you, Molly. You made it all possible. I would be dead if it wasn't for you. I missed you so fucking much that some days I wanted to pack up and go back to Cornwall and just be with you but I realised that I had to sort my shit, Molly. I had to work through everything, make amends, pay whatever fucking debt I needed to pay so that I could be the person you deserved."

"You were always that person," she buries her head in my chest, and I feel her tears through my shirt. "You had to do it for you, not for me."

"I did do it for me." I admit, "but you kept me going. In the darkest moments, when it was too painful to keep putting one foot in front of the other, I thought of you, and I got through it."

"You can't send me away again, Jonny, you have to promise, because for me, this is it. You are it..."

"You are my happily ever after, Molly!" I grin and lift her head so her eyes meet mine. "You're the one I've been looking for my whole fucked up life. It's you."

"Really?"

"Really!"

"How do you know."

"Because I fucking love you. I loved you from the first moment I saw you, from you puking in my bin to picking me up when I fell. I loved you then, I love you now and I'll love you forever."

"You could write the perfect song for a boy band you know," she says laughing, her eyes bright with tears.

"How to burst a rock star's bubble..."

She leans up and kisses me, the touch of her lips sending fire around my body. "I love you Jonny Raven, superstar, and I will love you for the rest of my life. I would have loved you even if we'd never met."

"I owe that journalist big time…"

"There is something you owe me first," she whispers running her fingernails up my thigh, "and we need to be alone for that."

"Damn woman!" I take her hand and lead her from the barn and out into the pouring rain. "Rain? For fucks sake!"

Molly laughs and opens her arms wide, spinning on the spot. "It's poetic, Jonny."

"Fucking annoying more like," I tug her arm and she wraps herself around me. "I suppose there is something serendipitous about it because it's not rained once since I've been here!"

"What can I say to that?" She laughs looking up at me, rain drops falling onto her lovely face before her expression becomes serious. "Did you mean it?"

"Mean what?"

"About forever."

"Forever and day…"

"Wow, that's a long time."

"You'd better believe it!"

A fork of lightening darts across the sky, flashing a bright white. I feel a weight shift and the remaining broken pieces inside of me fall into their place. I can stop running, stop searching, stop hoping because my journey has ended. I am no longer *the fucking little shit who should never have been born,* instead I am, and will always be, Jonny Raven. The future is bright, and for the first time in my life, I am safe. Molly reaches up for my face and kisses me, a kiss filled with all the promises of the future. The rain hammers down but there, under the stormy sky, I am finally whole. She is here and I am home.

To be continued...

The final instalment of the Stormy Skies series is
coming…

Author's Note

There is a feeling, just before the final few words, which is breathtaking and I often get up, move around, do anything other than type the last couple of sentences, because I'm just not ready to let the story go. It has been the same with Electric Dreams – the journey I went on with Molly and Jonny has been all-consuming. Their story was meant to start and end with Broken Ballads, but the characters had other ideas and a final instalment is coming!

Thank you for reading Electric Dreams, and hopefully you have loved it too. Keep your eye on my socials for updates on the final book in the trilogy, and if you have the time, please do leave a review.

Love Katie xxx

Ps – Typos and geographical inaccuracies are all mine!

Socials
Insta – katiejanenewmanwriter
Facebook – facebook.com/katienewmanauthor
Threads – katiejanenewmanwriter
Website – www.katiejanenewman.co.uk

Printed in Great Britain
by Amazon

27336906R00118